The OVERKILLING THE PAST trilogy is available now

BOOK 1

Overkilling the Past

BOOK 2

WHAT COMES AROUND The Story of Karma

BOOK 3

Detective Lucas: End of an Error

WHAT COMES AROUND The story of Karma

Copyright ©⯑ 2025

William L. Ash

ISBN: 979-8-9926441-2-8

Printed in the United States * Irving, Texas 75038

Ashfam Publishing

Contact: Leeash35@yahoo.com

First, let me just say that I am absolutely aware of the time investment needed to sit down and read a book. So, before you start this one, I want you to know how humbling it is and how appreciative I am that you chose this one to read.

Thank you.

Next, although I use my friend's names in my stories, they are nothing like the characters they share their names with.

Previously on Overkilling The Past...

Everything was going just fine for me, life was good. Not so much for my wife, Patricia. She didn't like our new place. She didn't have friends, and she hated her new job.

Her normally happy face became a resting b-word face. (Pardon my French.) Gone was the happy-go-lucky charm and the small town cheer, replaced by sharp tongued sarcasm, quick anger, and mean spirited put downs.

It all came to a head after we had a decent night drinking at an out of the way bar and grille. I was too drunk to drive my truck, so my job was to play the in-car DJ from the passenger seat.

Calling her a cautious driver was me being generous to my wife. Nervous was a better word... She just drove too slow. Cars always beeped and honked and passed us. It wasn't a big deal. But on this night, there was a guy who kept flashing his high beams, yelling out of his window, and tailgating us. Enraged, she slammed on the brakes, causing him to run into the back of my truck.

"Uh oh, better get Maaco," I laughed, amused in my drunken state.

In one quick motion, she grabbed my pistol from the glovebox, my knife from the door pocket, got out, and walked back to the vehicle that hit us. All of this as I clumsily struggled to untangle myself from my seat belt.

Finally freed, I got out.

POP! POP!

I saw the fire from the gun barrel light up his car's interior, then saw her doing a repeated punching motion.

The two shots killed him, the additional stabbing was just overkill.

"Get back in the truck," she said as she walked calmly back towards me.

"Wait, what just...?"

"GET BACK IN THE FUCKING TRUCK!"

Then, 9 years later...

WHAT COMES AROUND

AROUND

The story of Karma

WILLIAM L. ASH

We are family, I got all my sisters and me! - Sister Sledge

Prelude

It was a cool September morning. Wednesday. The sky was a perfect, clear blue. There was a light breeze that said summer's on its way out, and fall is on its way in.

Karma Lucas stepped outside of a two bedroom apartment and looked up, shocked to see a bird fly into the window of the place she'd just left. It fell to the ground, twitching, flopping around, trying to get up. Its neck was broken. Karma hurried over and picked it up.

"What's wrong, little bird? What happened?" She tried to support its head as she held it close, trying to comfort it. The bird continued to twitch and flutter its little wings.

"Do you need help flying? Do you need Mama to help you fly?" she asked, assuming the role of the bird's parent.

"Here! Fly then!" Karma flung the bird as high up in the air as her muscles allowed, then stepped back and watched it fall right back down to earth, splattering bird blood on the pavement.

"What's wrong with you, dumb bird!' she yelled, "Fly! Fucking fly!" She reached down bare-handed, grabbed the bird, and threw it up in the air again. "FLY!" she screamed.

Splat!

"That's not how birds work, love," Patricia Brown, Karma's best friend, said, coming from the apartment, shutting the door behind her. "Come on, you can't afford to be late again. You're gonna get fired!"

"Ok, lady, I'll see you there," Karma said.

Patricia rubbed her friend's shoulder as they parted and headed to her car at the end of the road. Karma stared down at the dead bird with a tear in her eye.

"Why didn't you fly? I tried to help you," she whispered.

Honk honk

"KARMA! GIRL, LET'S GO!" Patricia yelled from her car as she drove by.

Karma waved, then ran across the street, narrowly missing being run over by an orange Mustang.

Honk! Honk!

"MOVE BITCH!" someone yelled.

"FUCK YOU! LEARN HOW TO DRIVE ASSHOLE!" She yelled back. "332 HJL. 332 HJL." She repeated the license plate number until she got in her car and entered it into the reminder app on her phone. "I got your bitch right here," she mumbled to herself as she did.

Karma took one last look at the apartment building, specifically, the window of the place where she and Patricia had left a man's mutilated body lying on his kitchen's linoleum floor.

CHAPTER 1: Introduction

It wasn't a surprise to Karma that she arrived to work at the same time as her friend, even though she'd left several minutes after. Patty was a notoriously slow driver. It frustrated Karma to the point that they often took two vehicles when going to the same place, Patricia being too nervous to ride shotgun.

She loved her friend, though. They were two peas in a pod, sistas from different mistas, birds of the same feather, and every other synonym that meant they were as close as siblings.

Patricia was the older, more cynical, more experienced, and put together of the two. Karma was the wide-eyed, overly optimistic, ambitious one. Although Karma's personality was often unpredictable and spontaneous, it was Patty who was the more violent and quick to anger. Karma was the brains, Patty was the brawn. They were thunder and lightning, the perfect storm.

"Hey girl, heeey," Karma said, laughing and throwing her middle finger up through the driver's window at Patty. She cut her off with her car and beat her into the 'closest to the door' parking spot.

She laughed again seeing her friend mouth the word 'bitch', then pull off to go find somewhere else to park.

This was the same spot where they met. It was Karma's first day, and both were in a hurry. Patricia had been waiting patiently for a different car to leave the space with her blinker on when Karma zoomed in from the other direction and stole it.

"Um, excuse me, that was my spot?" Patricia said, through her window, as politely as she could at that hour of the morning.

"Was, being the key word," Karma replied with too much attitude.

Patricia put her car in park, then got out, moving aggressively towards the younger woman, who matched the aggressiveness with her own. "What, grandma? You snooze, you lose!" she snapped her fingers, putting an exclamation point on her statement.

"Look, bitch..." Patty started to say before being interrupted by Jared, who greeted them both with a pleasant, "Good morning, ladies. How are y'all doing on this fine morning?"

"Good morning, Jared," Patricia said, instantly relaxing her attitude.

"Good morning, sir. I'm fine, thank you," Karma replied, before returning her attention to the woman without a parking spot.

"Look, I have to go, it's my first day and I don't want to be late. Next time, move quicker. I got here first. You know how I know that I got here first? Because I'm already parked and you're standing out here having hot flashes in the cold. Is this how menopause looks? Cuz it don't look good. Ugh!" She grabbed her things and walked away, leaving Patty standing there, staring daggers into the new hire's back.

"Karma's a bitch you know!" she called out.

"No, I'm actually not," the younger woman said to herself.

Karma made her way inside, met with a few other new hires she remembered from orientation, then found a seat in meeting room A, where she excitedly waited for her instructor, enthusiastic, ready to start this new journey.

That's when the woman from the parking lot walked in.

"Hello, I'm Assistant Plant Manager Patricia Brown. Not Patty, not Pat, Patricia. I'll accept Miss Patricia, or Mrs. Brown, that's it. Does everyone understand?" she said, taking instant command of the room. "You!" she pointed at Karma, "stay after this meeting. We need to talk."

That was 2 years ago. They've been besties ever since.

"Hey! Remember when we met? Ha ha. I stole your spot. Ha ha. You were so mad," Karma teased, skipping along.

"Stop," Patty warned.

"You were like, Karma's a bitch motherfucker! Ha ha ha!" Karma continued.

15

"It wasn't funny."

"Yes, it was. You was like, grrr, grrr, meet me after the meeting. Grrr."

This was Karma. Light, easy, playful.

"Oh my God, Karma, Stop. You're giving me a headache! I swear if you were somebody else, I'd... " This was Patty. Especially at work.

Karma clocked in, Patty didn't need to; she was salaried.

"I have a new one," Karma said, after calming down. "I'll send you the details."

Patty walked away. They couldn't be best friends at work. She had responsibilities. She had an image to uphold. She was the ice queen, Miss unflappable, that bitch in the corner office. She offered Karma a slight smile, and they went their separate ways.

Beep Beep Beep

It was after lunch when the text came across her phone.

'Peppermints, we're on the news!'

Peppermints was the favorite nickname Karma had for her, even though she insisted that she didn't like to be called out of name.

Exhaling her frustration, she picked up her phone and clicked on the link.

Exonerated priest found mutilated and castrated in his apartment. *Police discovered the body in a gruesome scene amid hundreds of photographs of his alleged victims. Captain Jefferson called the scene the most horrific thing he'd ever witnessed. The priest was in....*

Patty put her phone down. She didn't need to read the rest of the article, she was there.

Beep Beep Beep

'Did you see it?' a text from Karma.

'Yes.'

'Good job, partner. I'll show you the new one tonight. I'm so tired today. This bitch Lisa is so annoying, can you fire her? I'm going to beat her ass. Seriously.'

Patty set her phone down, finished with the conversation.

Chapter 2: Three women and a baby

Patricia Brown went home after work to cook for her husband Charles, prepare his work clothes for the next day, then left to meet Karma at Buggsy's, a restaurant near downtown. She saw her friend sitting at the bar with two wine glasses in front of her.

"Thanks," Patty said, grabbing the closer of the two glasses, and sitting down.

"Um, no! Those are both for me. I need it after today!" Karma joked, "Our bartender is right there. Get your own."

Patty looked directly in Karma's eyes as she took a sip, daring her to say something about it.

Karma waved her hand and said, "Whatever," as they both laughed. "Anyways, I got this new case. Drunk driver, 3 out of a family of four dead, the only survivor was a 5-year-old girl."

"So? That happens all the time, what's the big deal?" Patty asked.

"He's a repeat offender, this is his 4th crash. He's a fortunate one, a senator's son." Karma sat back for effect, waiting to be recognized for her clever use of the song lyric. Patricia didn't pick it up, so she continued. "He jumped bail, but I know where he's..."

Karma wanted to be a detective like her dad. She found a website on the dark web called the Bounty Hunter's Bible that listed the names and crimes of bad people who either skipped out on bail or were let off easy, with their light sentencing disproportionate to the weight of their crime. There was a payout for every person caught. She didn't care about the money, though; she just wanted to prove herself worthy. It was like she was still fighting for her father's attention.

Dewayne Lucas was a detective best known for being on 48 Hours, a popular reality TV show that would follow real life detectives doing their jobs, trying to solve murder cases. The hook was that the odds of finding the suspect lessened after 48 hours.

One case in particular involved the detective, Karma, and her mom, Keisha Lucas. It started with her and her mom being kidnapped, then watching her kidnapper get shot and tossed over a cliff right in front of her. It ended with her mom being shot in the head, her dad being handcuffed to a tree, then her being taken hostage, but eventually being set free.

Everything changed that night.

With her mom gone, it was just Karma and her dad. The case turned him into a megastar. He went from being a regular officer to America's top detective. He quit the force and the TV show to start doing consulting work around the country. Everybody loved him. He went from being a husband to the world's most eligible widower. Karma got lost in the shuffle and was forced to spend most of her time at her grandmother's house. Her father went from being a dad to just a guy on TV.

The worst part about it was the fact that the real killer was never caught. The reports that came out through the news and media were that the man who kidnapped them, shot her mom, and was then killed by Detective Lucas. But that wasn't true. There was a 3ʳᵈ, unmentioned man. That man was the only killer. He was the one who shot her mom and the kidnapper.

Karma could never understand why her dad never said anything about him. She remembered him talking to the man as if they were friends, yet when she asked her dad about it, he said she was imagining things. He said that the trauma caused her young brain to misremember what really went down.

He was wrong, though; she remembered everything about that night. She remembered exactly what the man looked like, the sound of his voice, the smell of his cologne, and the look in his eyes. To her, it was like everything just happened yesterday. She wouldn't admit to herself that her father lied; he was a good man, but he didn't tell the whole truth.

Fast forward some years, and unable to pass the physiological part of the police officers' enrollment test, plus being deathly afraid of firearms, she couldn't become a real detective. Bounty Hunter's Bible was her only way to satisfy what she called her true calling. It helped to pacify the longing she had for her father.

"Helloooo? Earth to Karma..." Patty said, waving her hand, snapping Karma out of the daze she was in.

"So, he's been staying with one of his side piece whores, on the south side. Celeste, (their mutual friend), did some digging and got an address," Karma said without missing a beat, not acknowledging the fact that she had just stopped talking mid-sentence a few seconds ago.

"Let's go get him," Patty said, standing.

"Ok, it's about 15 minutes from here, so if you leave now, I'll finish my drink, get one more, then use the restroom and meet you at the address. You should be just about there by then," Karma said, half-jokingly.

"Hardy har, bitch!" Patty responded, laughing. "You drive."

"I love you Peppermint Patttttyyy!" Karma teased.

They drove to a neighborhood on a side of town where you wouldn't typically find a senator's son.

"Nice place to hide," Patty said, looking around at the run-down houses of the low income area.

"There it is, right there," Karma said, pulling up in front of the apartment.

Patty put her hand in her purse, on a pistol that her husband gave her on Valentine's Day. Karma looked at it, then looked away. She hated that her friend carried it, but knew that it was a necessary evil.

They got out and walked to the front door, Karma as usual taking the lead. She knocked politely, then waited. No answer, she knocked again. This time they could hear movement inside, then a middle-aged woman opened the door carrying a baby in one hand, a cellphone in the other, and had a cigarette hanging from her nicotine stained lips. The tiny studio apartment reeked of old tobacco, as a thick cloud of smoke hung heavy in the air. Both women coughed before Karma spoke.

21

"Hi, sorry to bother you so late, but I'm looking for Brandon Jefferson…" She barely got the words out when the woman slammed the door in their faces.

Karma knocked again, harder than she had moments earlier. The woman swung the door open aggressively, "WHAT! WHAT THE FUCK DO YOU…"

Karma snatched the baby from her arms before she finished her sentence, as Peppermint Patty punched the woman in the face and pushed her back into the room, knocking her down. Karma tossed the baby on the couch and then jumped on top of the fallen woman. Patty grabbed the cellphone, pressed end, hanging up on whoever was on the line, then threw it on the ground and stomped it into a thousand pieces.

Karma smacked the woman repeatedly, then put her face unnecessarily close, until her mouth touched the ear of this person she'd never met before. She whisper-screamed at her, "WHERE THE FUCK IS BRANDON? WHERE THE FUCK IS BRANDON? WHERE THE FUCK IS BRANDON?"

"HELP! HELP ME! STOP! GET THE FUCK OFF OF ME!" the woman yelled.

Karma put her hand over her mouth. Patricia picked up the screaming baby and bounced it gently, trying to get it to stop crying, "Shhhh, Shhhh!"

"Hey mama… It's ok, I know you're scared," Karma spoke soothingly while patting the woman's hair. "But we're not here to hurt you." She stood, then helped the bleeding woman to her feet and sat her on the couch. The woman reached for her cigarette first, then her baby.

Patricia looked at Karma, biting her lip. Karma shook her head, no.

"Tell us where Brandon is and we'll leave. What's your name, love?"

Through tears, the woman answered, "Ronda." She put out the cigarette she was smoking, then lit another.

"Ok, Ronda, where is Brandon?" Karma asked again calmly.

"He's ... he's..." Ronda stammered.

"HE'S WHAT? FUCK, RONDA! SNAP OUT OF IT! WHERE IS BRANDON!" Karma screamed. She looked back at Patricia, who was rocking back and forth on her heels, ready to pounce.

"He's at Cabana House, downtown, watching the game, alright? Ok? I told you where he is, now go!" Ronda said.

Karma stood and grabbed a handful of the woman's hair, pulling her up, making her stand, then kissed her softly on the cheek, "Was that so hard? Why'd you have to make it so difficult, love?" She patted Ronda on the butt then walked out followed by Patricia.

Cough! Cough!

The baby coughed twice. The sound of phlegm in the child's throat stopped Patricia in her tracks.

"Nooo!" Karma begged her friend, "Let's go, please…"

Peppermint Patty turned and pushed her way back inside. She pressed her pistol hard into Ronda's forehead and told her to put the baby down. Karma closed the door, then waited outside, not wanting to witness what was about to happen.

Peppermint Patty pushed Ronda by the neck, hard up against the refrigerator, finally putting her gun back in her purse.

She noticed a plastic grocery bag that was hanging from a cabinet and put it over Ronda's head. The woman didn't fight back, like she was used to violence.

Patricia lit 3 cigarettes, blew the smoke into the bag, then squeezed it shut over the woman's head.

"Breathe bitch! This is how that baby feels trying to breathe your nasty cigarette smoke," she growled.

Ronda finally started to struggle… She was holding her breath.

Patricia kneed her in the stomach, and repeated herself, "Breathe! How's it feel? How do you like secondhand smoke? How do you think that baby feels? TELL ME!" She let go of the bag just long enough to blow more smoke into it, then squeezed it closed again.

Ronda was dying, the baby was screaming, but Peppermint Patty was perfectly at peace in the chaos. Karma burst through the door and grabbed her friend, stopping her from killing the innocent woman.

"Enough," she said, "enough. She's not our target. She's not why we came... Come on, please, she's had enough."

Patricia looked at her, then at the baby, then at Ronda. She let go of the bag, shook her head, and walked outside without a word.

Karma looked down at the woman who was now lying on the ground, coughing and gasping for air. She opened her mouth to speak, but didn't.

She started to walk outside to her car, where Patty was already sitting in the passenger seat, but stopped to put the crying baby's pacifier in its mouth.

"I'm sorry, little one," she whispered.

Chapter 3: Peppermint Patty

The two friends rode together in silence. Karma, not knowing what to say, Patty not wanting to talk.

Karma stole glances at her friend and saw the same look of determination that she always saw. Patty always looked straight ahead, she always knew exactly where she was going. She wasn't the type who got distracted by shiny things. If she went to the store for toothpaste, then toothpaste was the only thing she'd buy.

Karma was the exact opposite. She could be doing a Google search on the weather, see an ad at the top of the page, and end up buying an automatic litter box for a cat she doesn't even have. Just in case she found a stray.

Karma envied her friend's focus and determination. She hoped that one day her life would be as complete and fulfilled when she was that age.

Patricia sat still, not wanting to admit that she'd lost her cool at the apartment. The coughing baby got her. It reminded her of motherhood and how she would protect her babies at all costs, and how today's moms seemed to take the blessing of birthing a child for granted. Certain things just released a rage in her that she couldn't always control.

She tried to remain calm and cool, calculated for karma's sake. She loved Karma and appreciated her friendship. She wanted to be that stoic, unwavering rock for her, so she always had someone to lean on. Patricia would always try to be by her side.

Their friendship was deeply personal but also distant. Patricia kept her at arm's length. Karma had never met her husband and knew very little about the intimate details of her. She knew that Patricia and her husband moved around a lot because of his job. She also knew that Patricia's rage came from an abusive childhood.

They did bond over both having lost their moms at a young age.

During a drunken girl's night out, after all the other girls left, Patricia admitted to having killed her father. Karma sat in shock as Patricia spoke...

"I was very shy when I was younger because of the shame I carried around. The abuse that me and my siblings went through just makes you... less... if that makes sense. So, my confidence was low, my self esteem was shit, and I just couldn't connect with people. I preferred to just be alone and tried to blend into the background. Of course, people thought I was weird, so I was picked on mercilessly through my teen years and early twenties.

Anyways, I went to a community college so I could be close to home for my siblings, and would often study at a local bar and grille after work. I would just sit there for hours and watch all the 'cool kids' drink and laugh, and joke around. I tried to stay unnoticed.

Charles noticed me, though. He worked there... bartender, dishwasher, handyman... He was nice to me. We talked and laughed and got along really well. He was kind of a loner too, but we differed in the way that he wanted to hang with the in crowd, I did not.

Long story a little longer, we ended up having sex and his 'friends' made a big deal out of it, so he did the classic 'I fucked you as a joke' thing, cuz of his little boy ego.

It hurt, I won't lie, but I knew what it was. He was trying to fit in. He was a square peg in a round hole."

"So, how'd you end up married?" Karma asked, hanging on to every single word.

"Well, he came and found me the next day, and we talked. He apologized and confessed that he killed the leader of the cool kids group for me."

"What?"

"Yeah, the crazy thing about it... I wasn't mad. I actually thought it was so romantic. I already liked Charles, but that, somehow just, I don't know, took it to the next level. Anyways, after a little bit, I told him about my abusive past, so he went to confront my abuser."

"Your dad?"

"Yes, my dad. Charles attacked him, and I helped. I cut a thousand holes in that motherfucker's dick!"

"Like the priest..." Karma added.

"Worse."

The two women sat in silence, deep in thought, before Patricia said, "And I liked it. The satisfaction of retribution for all my years of suffering made me want to do it more. But I wanted to help people. I wanted to... I don't know, be Karma."

She looked at her friend, who sat wide-eyed in awe.

"I remember the first time I did one alone. I had applied for a job at a nursing home, and when I walked in, something was off. I couldn't place it, but the way that the staff was acting... I don't know, they were laughing and having fun, it was weird for a nursing home. Anyways, I had a good interview on the 2nd floor, and as I was leaving, when I stepped into the elevator, there was an elderly lady, but the two other people, a man and a woman, were standing there giggling. They were trying to hold in laughter. The old lady jumped at me, begging, "HELP! PLEASE? TAKE ME WITH YOU! PLEASE!" I didn't understand, but when I asked if she was ok, the man said she was just loopy from her meds. I told them to leave her alone and went to report them. The girl told me "To mind my own business, bitch." I left but waited 4 hours until their shifts were over. I saw her come out and I followed her. When she opened her car door, I stabbed her in the neck. She fell, and I poked like, a hundred 6-inch holes in her face. She squealed like a pig when I cut her tongue out of her disrespectful mouth."

"Oh my God, she was still alive? What about the guy?"

"I got him too, I didn't mean to, though. He came outta nowhere and tried to defend her. He grabbed my arm. I accidentally stabbed him like, 20 times, then left them on the ground together. They looked so sweet lying there like Romeo and Juliet," Patricia said nonchalantly, finishing the last few drops of her drink and setting her glass on the table. "You ready to go?"

"You ready? Hey! Patty cakes! You ready? We're here," Karma was saying impatiently.

Patricia snapped out of her daze and looked around. She was so lost in her memory, she didn't realize that they were already sitting outside of Cabana House.

"There he is!"

They watched him stumbling across the parking lot, drunk, towards his car.

Karma pulled up next to him as Peppermint Patty grabbed her pistol and got out.

"Hey!" She pistol whipped him, then grabbed him by the arm with the gun to his head.

"Let's go Brandon."

Chapter 4: Walk it off

"Wait! Let go of me! Who the hell do you think you are? Get your goddamn hands off me!" An inebriated Brandon slurred his words.

"We're taking you in, you're going to jail!" Karma said.

"The hell I am. Do you know who I am?" he asked. His arrogance on full display.

Patricia shoved him in the backseat, then sat down next to him, gun pointed at his temple. Karma got in on the other side, and they quickly zip tied his wrists.   "HELP! HELP! I'M BEING KIDNAPPED!" he yelled.

Patricia hit him in the face with her gun, "Shut up!"

"OW! You two are in so much trouble. Ha ha. You just messed with the wrong person." Brandon bled from his face.

Karma got in the driver's seat and started driving towards the police station.

Brandon grew more agitated the longer they drove. He started kicking the seats, hollering, and violently throwing a tantrum like a 2-year-old. He spat at Karma, which earned him another hit to his already battered face.

"Pull over, I've had enough," Peppermint Patty said.

Karma did as her friend asked.

Patricia got out first, then grabbed him by his wrists. "Get out!" she demanded. "You don't want to ride like a normal person, you can walk." She looked up and down the empty stretch of roadway. "Pop the trunk," she told Karma, who had joined them on the side of the road.

Patricia grabbed a tow rope. She connected one end of it to the bumper, and the other end, she secured it with extra zip ties to his hands. "Let's go," she told Karma and got into the driver's seat.

"HEY! HEY! WHAT THE HELL ARE YOU DOING? TAKE THIS FUCKING THING OFF ME! NOW!" Brandon's bravado disappeared. It was replaced by fear.

Karma reluctantly got in the passenger seat. "Ummm, what's going on exactly?" she asked nervously.

"He didn't want to act right and ride like a normal person, so he's going to walk. He asked to be let out, he's out," Peppermint Patty said matter of factly, shifting the car into drive.

She eased the car to a snail's pace of 5 miles an hour. Brandon screamed for her to stop. He continued to switch between apologies and demands. She moved up to 10 miles an hour when she heard him call her a bitch.

"Ok, ok... alright, he gets it. Let's stop now, he gets it," Karma pleaded, worried. She kept looking back from Brandon to Patricia, her face had a look of horror.

"I'M GONNA KILL BOTH OF YOU BITCHES WHEN I GET OUT OF THIS!" he yelled.

Patricia did a quick step on the gas, causing the car to leap forward, which in turn caused Brandon to fall.

"STOP! OH MY GOD, HE FELL. PATTY, STOP!" Karma was about to have a meltdown.

"What? What are you saying?" Peppermint Patty asked, acting innocent.

"AAAAHHHHH!" Brandon had been dragged 5 feet after he fell. "STOOOOP!" Please, stop," he cried.

"Oh my God!" Karma was out of breath. "Patty…"

Peppermint Patty watched Brandon stand up through the rearview mirror. His clothes were torn, and all of his exposed skin, including his face, was scratched up and bloody. He bent over, crying, trying to catch his breath. She put her foot back on the gas pedal and slowly started to move again.

"NO!" Karma screamed.

"HEY! STOP! I CAN'T. I CAN'T DO IT!" he yelled, as he started to jog, terrified of being dragged again.

Patricia had been dragged before. Her mind went back to her chubby 13-year-old, 7th grade self.

She was older than her classmates because she failed 7th grade the first time through. She was smart enough, but missed too many days of class. Her father wouldn't let her go to school with all the bruises she often had, for fear that they would accuse him of child abuse. His discipline was severe.

On the night before her last day of school, he sent her and her brother to the corner store for potato chips and a bottle of Mountain Dew. He told them they had exactly 9 minutes and 45 seconds. Any later was trouble.

Her brother Martin was the quarterback of the football team, 4 years older than her. Their dad thought it would be funny to tether them together with a piece of rope.

She loved Martin. She looked up to him. He did everything he could to protect her, but he was no match for their father.

"Come on, let's jog," he said, putting his arm around her, "We'll be ok."

The jog to the store was hard for her. She wasn't an athlete, she didn't have the physical tools that her brother had. They got to the store in 3 minutes, but it was a struggle. They bought their stuff and had time to get home, but halfway back, she just couldn't jog anymore.

"Wait," she said, out of breath, "Please." Her lungs were on fire. Her heart was beating so hard, she thought it was going to explode.

"Put your hands on your hips, breathe easy, and walk. You'll be ok," her brother insisted.

"Ok," she said. And she tried. She really did, but just couldn't keep up. The leash made it worse because he was pulling, hurting her back, squeezing her diaphragm, shortening her air supply.

"Patricia, come on!" Martin was getting irritated. His lead was getting further and further, which put more tension on the rope.

"I'm trying," she cried, "I'm trying." She felt like she was going to faint.

Time was running out. They had 1 minute 45 seconds left but were only 1 minute away.

"Please, 30 seconds… just give me 30 seconds, then I'll sprint. Please."

"No, Patty, let's go!" he urged. She stopped anyway. He started to drag her. It hurt. She fell and started to cry. "Hey! Stop! I can't. I can't do it!"

"PATRICIA! LET'S GO!" he yelled, physically dragging her across the grass of the field they were crossing. "GET UP! FUCK! YOU FAT PIG, GET UP!"

His words broke her heart. That's what their dad always called her. That's what everyone called her. Everyone except for him. He was the only one who stood up for her. He was the only one who treated her like a person. He was the only one who cared.

"OK! OK!" she said, standing, "OK." She jogged back home. They made it but barely, at 9 minutes, 30 seconds. She fell on the porch, out of breath, dying, as her brother untied their leash, then went inside to give their dad his stuff.

She thought she was passed out until she heard yelling. She got up and went inside to find her dad hitting her brother with a belt.

"Wait! Stop! We were on time, we made it, we were on time. What's happening?" she cried.

"No. He, made it on time. You were outside. You and your fat belly were sleeping on the porch. You were both supposed to be here, at 9:45. He's a bad brother. He should've brought you in!" their dad explained.

Her brother closed his eyes as he was being hit.

"STOP! PLEASE STOP! IT WAS MY FAULT! STOP HITTING HIM. HE MADE IT. IT WAS MY FAULT! PLEASE, STOP!" she screamed at her father.

He stopped swinging his belt and stared at her. He took a step towards her, but Martin stepped in between them, refocusing her dad's attention back on him. He was her hero. The older man grabbed him, spun him around, then had both of Martin's arms twisted up, in a full nelson. His shoulder was locked out, pulled around his own neck, choking, in a sleeper hold position.

"STOOOOP! DAD, PLEASE!" she yelled.

Snap!

Her dad broke her brother's arm and pulled the shoulder out of its socket. It was the first and only time she saw him cry.

"Walk it off, sissy," her fathered teased.

The injury ended Martin's football career. He never played another game.

Patricia lost her brother that night. He never spoke to her again. He would do head nods and point, but they never had another real conversation.

She suffered from nightmares for years after that, but could never remember the details. Just that she would always wake up screaming, "STOOOOP!"

"STOOOOP! PATTY, WHAT THE FUCK! STOP!" Karma grabbed the emergency brake, stopping the car.

Patricia looked around as if she had just woken up. She didn't even recognize who Karma was at first.

"What? What happened?" She was in shock.

"WHAT IS WRONG WITH YOU! OH MY FUCKING GOD!" Karma said, getting out of the car, slamming her door.

"WAIT! What did I do? I blacked out." Patty got out to follow her friend. "What did I do?"

Karma stood frozen at the back of the car. Her face was sheer horror. She looked at Patty, then turned and threw up. Patricia saw what Karma saw. She looked down at what used to be a human being. The tow rope was now only connected to a bloodied and mangled mess of flesh and bone. She had dragged Brandon until he was nothing more than roadkill, shredded meat for the birds. Shocked, she looked around, finally seeing where they actually were... A mile and a half from where they started.

Chapter 5: Avengers

The women didn't talk about what happened until after work the next day in the parking lot, when Karma said, "Hey, Miss Brown, do you have a minute?"

"I do. How can I help you, Miss Lucas? I love your hair like that, by the way," Patricia responded politely.

"Thank you, ma'am. And your meticulously applied makeup looks flawless as always, but I wanted to comment on your actions the other night. Unfortunately, they compromised the bounty," Karma said.

"They did, I know, and I sincerely apologize. I recognize the problem and am actively working towards a solution."

The two friends continued their overly polite argument.

"But our goal was to rid the streets of a certain miscreant; have we not satisfied our desired objective?" Patricia asked. "And was my understanding incorrect? I thought the motivation was justice, not monetary or financial gain."

"No, you were correct in your assessment, but the time I invested... You know what, fuck it, I put a lot of energy and effort trying to find this guy. What you did... what we did, wasn't justice, it was vigilanteism."

Patricia raised a skeptical eyebrow at the phrase.

"What?" Karma said, "That's a word."

Patricia shook her head doubtfully.

"It's a word, I'm pretty sure it's a word." Karma tried to sell it.

"It's not," Patty said in her authoritative tone.

"I think it…"

"Hey. It's not. Let it go, love." Patricia laid a comforting hand on her friend's shoulder.

"Ok. Fine. But you get my point. We are not the law. We bring them in so the authorities can do their jobs," Karma reasoned, "When you do what you did, all of my hard work is for nothing. It takes a lot to find these guys. Let the authorities do their job!"

"But that's the whole point. They're not doing their jobs! We are. You think the families of the victims give a damn if these assholes die? They don't. Nobody wants to waste tax money putting these losers away, giving them 3 hots and a cot. We are doing the world a favor."

Karma turned away, frustrated. She wondered if anyone was watching them argue in the middle of the parking lot and what they thought about it. She could already hear the rumors.

"Hey," Patricia said, changing the subject, "we need a name, like a team name. Something that represents us and what we do. Oooh, we can have hand signals. No, we'll wear special rings. Yes, like the Wonder Twins!"

"What?" Karma asked. "What does that even mean?"

"How about the Avengers?" Patty said, interrupting her friend. "Because we are avenging the victims for the families. YES! We'll be the Avengers."

"Wait a minute. What are you saying? The Avengers? Like the comic book movie?"

"Yes. Like we're heroes or something. That will be our gang name," Patricia continued excitedly.

"Gang name? What? Oh my God, I'm so confused. Patty cakes, what are you saying? Are you having one of your episodes?" Karma stood there, shaking her head.

Patricia held up her hand for an awkward high five, then walked away to her car, fist pumping the air, saying "Avengers!"

"Wait! I have..." Karma started to say before finishing with, "another case."

She walked to her car, wondering what had just happened. She smiled to herself, truly hoping that Patty was only joking about having a gang name. They were not a gang!

Although she laughed at the ridiculousness of it, she found herself thinking about what her gang name alias should be, as she drove away.

Killer Karma. *'No, I'm not a killer.'*

Karegiver Karma (with a K)! *'Ha ha, nobody's afraid of a caregiver... Come on... think! How would Patricia describe you?*

She pulled her car into a parking space at a grocery store, then sat, thinking way too hard, for way too long, about something she'd thought was silly to begin with.

"How would Patricia describe me?" she asked out loud.

"OH, BIPOLAR! I'll be Bipolar Bear! Ha!" She got out of her car laughing at how dumb that sounded, then grabbed her phone to Google the names of The Avengers characters.

'Carol Danvers, I like her. She is me.' She thought to herself, ready to text Patty about her new gang name. "Shit!" She dropped her purse, spilling all of its contents out. "Goddamnit!" she said, not mad, but frustrated.

"Here, let me help," a male voice said, kneeling, handing her her own personal items.

He looked familiar, but she couldn't place his face.

"This must be yours," she said, handing him a tampon.

He put it in between his fingers like a cigarette, then held it to his mouth, "It is, thanks! I been trying to quit. It's hard, though. Got a light?"

Karma laughed, then snatched her tampon back from him quickly before he could react.

"Whoa! That was quick, what are you, a ninja?" he said with a smile.

"No, I'm an avenger," she smiled back, standing, checking to make sure she had everything, then walking away. "Thank you!" she called over her shoulder without looking back.

She grabbed her basket and headed towards the back of the store to get some milk. And some paper towels. And some yogurt. Oh, and tortillas are on sale? She grabbed some tortillas.

She walked to the front, placed her basket in a cart, then went back to seemingly buy one of everything in the store. She stood in the produce section trying to decide if spending the extra 50 cents for organic bananas vs. the other bananas was worth the extra money.

"Isn't all fruit technically organic?" she said to anyone who could hear her.

"Yes and no. It's about the pesticides and chemicals. It's basically just saying that these were grown without anything synthetic," the man from outside said. "Hi. I'm Manuel." He held out his hand.

She looked at it, trying to decide if she wanted to shake it or not.

"My friends call me Manny."

"Hi Manuel, my friends call me Carol," she said, deciding to use her gang name.

"Ah, yes, the Avenger. I remember you. What's your superpower?" he asked politely.

"Disappearing," she said, walking away, but not before grabbing the non-organic fruit.

"Ha ha ha, ok Carol, nice to meet you," he said, watching the way her waist wiggled.

Standing in the self check out line, her thoughts went to the night before and the mess they made of Brandon's body.

It was going to give her nightmares. The way Peppermint Patty was so calm as she disconnected the tow rope, then drove over the carcass back and forth, over and over, until there was nothing but a stain on the concrete. Karma could still hear the crunching of bones and the sound of stickiness as the blood and the man's organs transferred from the tires to the street. She lost at least 8 pounds from vomiting so much and wondered if that's what those bulimic models felt like when they purged themselves after every meal. They went to a car wash after that, and even though they both contributed to the cleaning, neither spoke.

Karma waited patiently, not looking at anyone or anything in particular, until a woman at the checkout to her left caught her eye. Karma watched as she swiped 1 item, then put 2 in her bag. The woman was stealing!

Karma looked around to see if anyone else saw what she was seeing. Nobody appeared to notice. Her first instinct was to call the manager and report this thief, but considering what she and Patty did the night before, she thought it best not to attract any attention to herself. It burned a hole through her soul as the crime happened right in front of her.

The woman finished, grabbed her stuff, and headed for the door. Karma left her cart and, against her better judgment, followed the thief outside.

"Hey Sarah! Hey, wait up!"

The woman kept walking.

"Hey!" Karma ran up and tapped her on the shoulder, unsure of what she was going to do next.

"Me? You were talking to me? That's not my name," she said dismissively, continuing to walk.

"Hey, wait, I'm sorry, I thought I knew you," Karma said following her, "You remind me of a fucking crook I used to know. Her name was Sarah, and she stole shit from grocery stores."

"Well, that's not me, fuck off, leave me alone," the thief picked up her pace walking through the parking lot.

"Go put it back," Karma said, grabbing the woman's cart.

"Let go! Get away from me."

"PUT IT BACK! PUT THE SHIT BACK!" Karma yelled. She pushed the cart over. Groceries went everywhere.

"GODDAMN IT, WHAT THE HELL IS WRONG WITH YOU?" the woman yelled, picking up her stuff.

Karma stood and watched, then helped the lady retrieve her items. "I'm sorry. I just, I don't know, I... Here, let me help."

"No, fuck off!" The woman grabbed her gathered things, then walked away, leaving Karma standing, holding a gallon of milk.

"Here, you forgot this," Karma called out, watching the lady climb into an orange Mustang.

"Fuck you, keep it," the woman said as she started her vehicle and pulled out of her spot.

332 HJL. Karma recognized the car and the license plate. She ran towards it, screaming, "TAKE YOUR MILK! TAKE YOUR FUCKING MILK YOU STEALING BITCH!" She threw it at the car, watched it splatter across the windshield, then watched as the woman drove away.

"Why didn't you want your milk? I told you I was sorry..." Karma said quietly.

Chapter 6: Diana Prince and Princess Leia

Patricia rode with Karma to the police station to meet with Celeste. Celeste was their insider. The one who could access hard to find information, do license plate traces, and perform facial recognition. She and Karma had been friends since the academy, though Celeste passed where Karma failed.

They had planned to meet in the lobby, then walk across the street and have lunch at Chili's.

"We should make her an honorary Avenger," Karma suggested as they walked into the station.

"Good idea, I mean, she's just as involved as we are," Patty replied enthusiastically.

"But, hey, listen. This is serious, we have to talk about this. I can't overstate this or emphasize this enough." Karma pulled her friend close and looked deeply into her eyes.

"Your name can't be Katniss Everdeen."

"What? Why not?" Patricia asked, offended.

"It doesn't make sense. We're supposed to be Avengers, not..."

"Fine. I want to be Wonder Woman then," Patricia replied defiantly.

"No. What? Have you even watched the movie?" Karma couldn't tell if her friend was joking or not. "You know the difference between DC and Marvel, right?"

"Fine, I want to be Storm, final answer," Patty said.

"What about Natasha Romanoff?" an uninvited male voice chimed in.

"WHAT?" Both women looked at him, irritated.

"Black Widow..." he started to say before being cut off.

"First of all, mind your business. Second, nobody asked you, mind ya business. Bye!" Patricia snapped.

"But..." he tried to explain.

"BYE!" she said again, louder.

Celeste came around the corner, surprised to walk into a commotion.

"Hey guys, what's happening? What's going on?" she asked, looking around at everyone. "Girls, have you met Detective Manuel?"

The detective extended his hand to Karma first, "Hello, call me Manny, please."

"Yeah, we met at the grocery store," she told her friends. "Hello again, Manuel. Detective, Manuel."

He smiled, "Hi Carol," then turned his attention to Patricia, extending his hand to her.

"This is Diana," Karma said before her friend could speak. "Diana, this is Detective Manuel. He's the one who left his number on my windshield instead of just asking me for my number, like a real man would."

"I thought you said he was a gentleman. Gentlemen don't interrupt people's conversations." She ignored his handshake. "Y'all ready?" She turned and walked out without another word. Her friends followed, leaving the detective standing there with his hand out.

"Who is he, and more importantly, who is Diana?" Patricia asked after they were seated and ordered.

"Diana is Diana Prince. Wonder Woman," Karma answered. "I figured we'd just go with that since you obviously have no concept of the different universes this Avengers gang is supposed to represent." She smiled sarcastically. She wasn't a comic book nerd by any means, but she at least knew that much.

"Oohh, ok, so I want to join your Avengers gang, and I want my gang name to be Princess Leia," Celeste said excitedly.

"Oh my God, you know what? Check please... I'm done." Karma grabbed her glass and tapped it with a fork while looking around for a waiter.

They all laughed. Karma still wasn't sure if they understood the joke. "Anyways, who is that detective? What's his story?" she asked. "He looks familiar to me."

"No story," Celeste began, "He came to us from out of state a couple of years ago. Nice enough guy... He does his job and goes home. I never seen him at any group events, but he seems to get along with everyone. I've never heard anyone say anything bad about him."

"I don't like him," Patricia said in a manner that meant she wasn't going to change her opinion.

"Who do you like, besides Charles?" Karma teased. She stuck her tongue out as she said it. She'd always thought it was odd that she'd never met Patricia's husband.

For two people who've shared so many emotional experiences, you'd think they would share everything, especially the most intimate details of their personal lives. For the hundreds of times Patty had been to her apartment, Karma had never gone to hers. She wasn't even positive about what city they lived in.

Of course, she could find out; she's a detective, but that was a line she would never cross. It was a breach of trust, and she valued her friendship too much to go digging through the woman's past. If Patty wanted her to know those things, she would tell her, if not, she wouldn't. Karma did her best to keep those feelings of exclusion pushed way back in her brain, to a space reserved only for her parents.

"Well, I've always been a fan of Princess Leia, but I am finally starting to like you too, Carol," Patricia said, answering the question. She reached out and touched her best friend's hand, then blew her a sarcastic kiss.

They shared another laugh.

"So, tell me what you got," Karma finally said.

"Yes, let's get down to business." Patricia sat up straight and deliberately stopped smiling.

Celeste started, "Good idea, I have to get back to work." She looked at her watch. " I found your couple, Robin and Steve, living 75 miles north of here on a 7-acre farm." She handed them each sheets of paper with the couple's pictures and bios.

"I forgot to ask her to run a trace on that license plate. Here, text her, tell her what I need." Karma said. She passed Patty her phone.

"Ok, done," Patricia said, passing it back.

"HEY! I KNOW THIS GUY!" Patricia said, riding shotgun in her fellow Avenger's car. "Charles used to love him, it was his favorite player. Has his jersey and everything. I thought he was dead, though. Didn't he die from some drug overdose or something?"

Karma didn't answer the rhetorical question. As soon as Patty mentioned Charles, her brain switched to a different place. They rode silently for a few miles towards the farm Celeste told them about before Karma finally said, "I think I'm gonna call him. I kinda like Detective Manny, he's ok, right?" She looked over at her friend, who already had her lips pursed.

"Girl, listen. You know that's not what you want. You got daddy issues, I get it, but don't just jump at every detective that's halfway nice to you. There's something off about him. You were right. Go with that first instinct, trust yourself. I know what you're going through, but trust me on this. Go with your gut." Patricia was being petty, and even though she knew that it came from the ridiculous feeling of jealousy that she had no right to, she didn't take it back.

Karma didn't respond.

Patricia looked to ease the tension in the car.

"YOUR MIND'S TELLIN YOU NOOOO. BUT YOUR BODY... YOUR BODY IS TELLIN YOU YEESSS. I KNOW YOU DON'T WANT TO HURT NOBODY..." She uncharacteristically started singing R Kelly's Bump and Grind out of nowhere.

Without missing a beat, they finished the lyric together, *"BUT THERE IS SOMETHING THAT I MUST CONFESS..."*

They had a good laugh. Karma looked over at her friend and smiled. She loved her Patty Cakes.

They followed the Google directions to a trail that was hidden just off the beaten path, which just happened to be located smack dab in the middle of nowhere. Patricia looked at the map to confirm what she already knew, "Yep, it says it right here, we're in BFE."

Without saying a word, they both knew that this was the part of the movie where the main characters should know better and turn around. Patricia had her pistol out on her lap, she was ready for anything, but if asked, she would admit that she didn't want to be there. All she could think about was the pig squealing scene in Deliverance.

They came to a clearing which opened up to a huge farmhouse to the left. There was a large barn to the right, with a long, winding driveway that split the two and led to a 2nd smaller barn.

Patricia couldn't hide her uneasiness with the situation.

"You ok?" Karma asked.

"It's just... I don't know... I have never been a pet person. I understand that people love animals. Some people love animals more than they love people. I get it. I've just never been that person. And this guy... Steve, the hall of famer. I mean, he's a national treasure. Do you know how many home runs he has? Do you know how many hits he has? We have his jersey hanging in our closet! Bat man. That's his nickname... I don't know... maybe we let this one pass," Patricia stared at the paper with Steve's picture on it.

"Yeah, well, he was also charged with the crime of animal cruelty. Did you see the pictures? He pleaded guilty. I don't have a pet either, never did, Grandma was allergic, but those poor dogs. They just... they were just so... And then this guy just acted like it didn't matter. The judge was a fan and decided to let Steve handle his affairs first, so everyone just expected that he would keep his promise to turn himself in. But wouldn't ya know, like magic, he poof! Just disappeared. Well, abracadabra bitch! The Avengers are here!" Karma paused for effect, then looked over at Patricia, who was already looking at her. "No?"

Patricia shook her head.

"I mean, it was a speech. Like, a motivational speech. You didn't feel it?" Karma asked.

Patricia shook her head again.

"But it was like..."

"Hey, no. It wasn't. I had to look around to see who you were talking to. Your voice changed and everything. I was thinking, 'Why is she talking like that?'" Patricia said.

"Really? I thought it was... whatever. Come on, let's go get your Batman," Karma said, getting out of the car.

"Ugh, they're just dogs..." Patricia replied, getting out reluctantly.

They walked a few steps towards the house when they were both hit in the face with the most vile, disgusting smell either of them had ever smelled.

It was the stench of rotted flesh and decaying bodies. They both looked in the direction of the smell through squinted eyes and saw a huge dog kennel surrounded by decrepit, crumbling, broken down dog houses, each with emaciated animals chained to rusted poles, covered in blood and feces. Some dead, some on the verge of dying.

There was a cage of healthier, but nowhere near healthy, dogs at the end of the pavement. They looked hungry and were crowded around a small pool of water when the women pulled up, but were now at the front, in a frenzy, barking and causing a ruckus.

"Oh my God!" Karma threw up and headed back to the car.

"Wait!" Patricia yelled, "Look!" She pointed. "Is that a..." She moved closer to get a better view.

"IT IS!," she looked back towards her friend, "it's a fucking kid! There's a kid in that fucking cage!"

Chapter 7: Batman and Robin

"Call 911! Now!" Peppermint Patty holstered her pistol and went towards the cage. Karma grabbed her phone and followed her friend.

The caged dogs were going crazy, barking, foaming at the mouth, fighting, and biting at each other, trying to get to the uninvited guests.

"Hey, kid, are you ok?" Patty yelled. The boy looked to be 6 or 7 years old and was just as skinny as any of the dogs. She reached for the door of the cage.

ZAP!

"Ow, fuck! It's electric. Tell them there's a child trapped in an electric cage!" she yelled.

"It's not working," Karma held up her phone, "it won't call out."

"That's because there's no signal out here. I got scramblers everywhere," said a male voice. "Who the hell are you, and what the hell are y'all doing on my property?" Steve came around the corner from the main house carrying a bat.

Normally, Patricia would have turned into a fan girl and ran over screaming, "Steve Vickson! Steve Vickson! Oh my God! I was there in 2019 when you hit the walk-off against the Rangers."

But Peppermint Patty didn't even acknowledge his existence. She was focused on the child who was taking advantage of the dogs being distracted enough to give him a chance to pick up scraps of food from the ground.

"Let the child out of the cage," she whispered, barely audible, as if speaking through her inner self.

"Hi, sir! Steve? Hey, I'm Carol, and that's Diana. Huge fans. I loved watching you dunk home runs through the field goal," Karma greeted him politely.

He towered over her and looked down before responding, "Get the hell off of my property!"

"Look, I need you to do two things for me," she said firmly. "1, let that boy out of that cage. And 2, put these handcuffs on and get in my car. We're taking you in for failure to appear."

"Let the child out of the cage," Peppermint Patty said, louder than before.

The dogs continued to make a ruckus.

"SHUT THE HELL UP YOU MANGY MUTTS!" Steve walked over to a pole and hit a switch that turned off the electricity to the cage. He grabbed a hose, then sprayed the dogs with high pressured water.

"SHUT UP! SHUT THE FUCK UP! ROBIN, GET OUT HERE! SHUT YOUR GODDAMN DOGS UP! ROBIN! GET YOUR ASS OUT HERE!"

The dogs cowered away from the water, but started barking again as soon as Steve stopped spraying them.

"LET THE CHILD OUT OF THE FUCKING CAGE! NOW!" Peppermint Patty demanded.

She turned and shot Steve in the knee.

POP!

"AAAAAAHHHH! YOU BITCH! YOU SHOT ME, YOU FUCKING BITCH!" he screamed.

She walked straight to the fallen man and pushed the gun hard against his forehead, finger on the trigger, ready to shoot again.

"NO! PAT-, DIANA, NO!" Karma ran over to them.

"No," she said with her hands up. "Stop!"

Robin appeared with a double-barreled shotgun and shot two rounds in the air.

BOOM! BOOM!

"WHAT THE HELL ARE YOUS DOIN ON MY PROPERTY!" she yelled, with an East Coast meets mid-west accent. She didn't seem too concerned with her husband when she said, "Get the hell away from my dogs!"

She aimed her gun at Patty, then Karma. Peppermint Patty didn't flinch. Karma ducked instinctively.

"Get off my land!" she yelled.

"Let the child out of the cage!" Patty countered, taking a step towards her.

"Get off, my land," Robin said adamantly, as if the first time she said it was more of a suggestion than a demand. She held the gun steady, now only pointing it at Patricia, who took another two steps.

"Back up!" she warned.

"Let the fucking child, out of the cage!" Peppermint Patty demanded.

"FUCK YOU! GET OFF MY LAND!"

"Patty! Stop!" Karma forgot to use their gang name. She jumped in between them, frantic, begging Robin, then turned around, pleading to Patricia. "STOP!"

Peppermint Patty took another two steps towards Robin, easily pushing past her friend.

There was a stalemate. Patricia put her forehead against the barrel of Robin's shotgun, daring her, while holding her own pistol aimed directly at the other woman's nose.

"Do it!" Peppermint Patty said calmly.

"Don't make me. I don't want to shoot you, but I will," Robin replied, moving her finger over the trigger.

"Do it, now! If you don't, I will," Patty promised.

"Don't. You. Fucking. Make me!" Robin jabbed the shotgun's barrel into Patty's forehead with each word.

"LET THE CHILD OUT OF THE FUCKING CAGE! NOW! FUCKING NOW!" Patricia yelled.

They stared at each other, unflinching, even as Steve hollered and Karma begged for them to put the weapons down.

The dogs were going absolutely crazy.

Robin had the trigger pulled back to its break point.

Peppermint Patty held her ground, fearless. She inhaled deeply, then released her breath slowly. She flinched. Robin squeezed.

Click!

Nothing happened.

Click! Click! Click!

Robin continued to squeeze the trigger, confused as to why it wasn't shooting. In one swift move, Patricia batted the shotgun out of her way with one hand and swung with the other, pistol whipping and knocking the woman to the ground.

Robin screamed in agony, holding her face as blood gushed through her fingers. Patty's gun fractured the woman's cheekbone, and a golf ball sized knot formed on the side of her head.

Karma ran to the fallen woman, begging, "Please. She's not gonna stop, just let the child out of the cage. She's going to kill you both!"

They looked over at Peppermint Patty, who was now standing over the whimpering Steve. He'd managed to drag himself halfway to the house. She pulled the man to his feet and kicked him in his shot leg. When he fell, she did it again. Her face wore a maniac's grin like she was having fun.

Karma turned back to Robin. "OPEN THE CAGE! OPEN THE CAGE! OPEN THE FUCKING CAGE!" she screamed. She had both hands around Robin's neck, squeezing the life out of her.

"OK... OK... I, I can't breathe," the woman tried to say. "Please... ok..."

Karma stopped, then helped her to her feet. Robin limped over to the switch they'd seen Steve use earlier and turned off the electricity.

Patricia now had Steve in a headlock, and was stroking her pistol in and out of his mouth as if he was giving it fellatio.

"Sit!" Robin said, standing at the fence. Every dog obeyed her command instantly.

"Back." They all moved simultaneously away from the cage's door.

"Gerald... Gerald, baby, come here. Come to mama," Robin said to the boy. He started to crawl to her. "Nooo, stand up. Two feet." The boy stood.

POP!

"AAAAAAAAHHHHH!!" Steve screamed.

"My bad!" Patricia called out. "My bad... that was my fault." She'd accidentally shot him in the hand. She looked over at Karma and shrugged.

"See? Look. The child is ok," Robin said. "Gerald is fine. He was just being a bad boy, huh? Bad boys have to sleep with the dogs, don't they?" Robin patted the boy's head affectionately, ignoring her husband's screaming. She looked at Karma, "Satisfied?"

Karma reached for the child and embraced him with a motherly hug, then slapped Robin across her bruised face.

"HE'S OK!" she yelled to her friend about the boy, "bring the Bat man over here." Peppermint Patty did as she was asked, leading the ex-baseball player by the hair.

"Batman..." Karma said, looking from him to his wife. "Batman and Robin... Oh shit! Batman and Robin! Ha ha ha ha! Oh my God! I didn't even realize. And we're Avengers! It's like a comic book scene. Oh my God!" Karma danced around doing the na na na na na, Batmaaaan. From the show's theme song. She bent down and kissed Robin on her broken cheek, then continued her song. Patricia checked on Gerald, making sure he was ok, then walked him back to the car and gave him a snack and a bottle of water. Satisfied that the child was ok, she went back to find Steve lying face down on the ground, with Karma sitting on his back, yelling, "FLY, BATMAN! FLY!"

Annoyed, Peppermint Patty said, "Batman doesn't fly, he's not a real superhero. Even I know that."

"Yes, he does," she replied, "he has a cape."

Karma stopped to think. "Why do you have a cape if you can't fly?" she asked Steve. She smacked him on the head. "ANSWER ME! WHY DO YOU HAVE A CAPE IF YOU CAN'T FUCKING FLY? WHY? WHY? WHY?" She bounced on his back as she smacked him on the head over and over again.

"ENOUGH KARMA! JESUS!" Patricia said, "You're giving me a headache."

Karma looked up with her feelings hurt.

"Put him in the cage," Patty decided. She turned and punched Robin hard in the stomach. When the woman fell, Peppermint Patty kicked her in the same spot she'd just punched.

"You don't deserve to be a mother! How could you put your baby in there? No more babies for you!" Enraged, she stood with her foot on Robin's midsection. "I SAID PUT HIM IN THE FUCKING CAGE! NOW!" she berated her partner, Karma.

"NO!" Steve yelled. "I hate dogs. Especially those worthless pieces of shit! Those are her dogs. Put her in the cage."

"Fuck you! You made them fight. You starved them and beat them and... You did that to those poor puppies!" Robin started to cry.

Patty lifted her foot.

"No, fuck you. This is your fault. All of this shit is your fault. You're the dog. You're a female dog! You lazy bitch, fuck you!" Steve was not the man Patricia thought he was. 'They say, never meet your heroes...' she thought to herself, making a mental note to throw away his jersey when she got home.

The dogs started barking again as Steve got closer to the door. They hated him. They foamed at the mouth, working themselves into a frenzy, wanting to get to him. Patty looked down at Robin with a look that said, 'You know what to do.'

Robin stood, painfully, then commanded the dogs to sit and be quiet, which they did instantly, as they kept their eyes trained on the man who'd abused and tormented them. They growled as he entered their cage.

"Wait, we can't just..." Karma started to say, as her friend, ignoring her, locked the cage, then turned on the electricity.

She reached over and grabbed Robin by the sleeve, pulling her to the car.

"STOP! WAIT! YOU CAN'T LEAVE ME HERE! WAIT A MINUTE! OK, I'LL GO WITH YOU. I'LL GO." Steve screamed angrily. The bass in his voice changed as fear crept in with the realization that the women weren't coming back.

None of the three turned to look, even as he continued to yell.

"LET ME OUT OF HERE! ROBIN! ROBIN YOU FUCKING BITCH! I WILL COME FOR YOU! I WILL KILL YOU! COME BACK HERE. NOW! YOU BITCH! YOU DIRTY, INBRED BITCH!"

Robin stopped at the car and finally turned to look at her husband.

"READY!" she yelled. The dogs all stood at attention simultaneously, waiting for their next command.

"SICK 'EM!"

CHAPTER 8: Keisha Lucas

The two friends were actually in good spirits on the way back to town. Even though they spoke demeaningly to Robin, who rode in the backseat with her son, there was a jovial sense about them.

Karma laughed, "You were like, Grrr! Grrr! Shoot me, I'll kill you. Ha ha ha. Oh my God, so funny!" She peeked in the rear view mirror as she drove, then looked over at Patricia, "You weren't scared?"

"Ha ha, no. Not at all. Those Banelli's... the shotgun she was holding,... it only holds 2 rounds at a time." She looked back at Robin, who was looking out the side window, sad and broken. "This idiot blew her wad before we even started to dance. Ha ha."

Karma looked in the backseat through the mirror. Robin carefully wiped a tear off of her broken face before saying, "Fuck you. Fuck you's both. Y'all don't know what I been through. You don't know what he did to us! Y'all don't fucking know anything about me! Fuck you!" She started to cry, pulling the boy closer to her.

"Stop!" Patricia ordered.

"Huh?" Karma was confused.

"STOP THE FUCKING CAR! REMEMBER BRANDON? STOP THE FUCKING CAR! NOW!" Peppermint Patty demanded.

Karma put her hand on her friend's leg and patted it, trying to calm her down.

"Shhh," she said mockingly. "Let it go. She just killed her husband, she's still emotional."

"I didn't kill my husband! You two psycho bitches did!" Robin cried alligator tears.

Peppermint Patty looked back, smirked, then turned up the radio. The women in the front seat sang along to Sister Sledge's We Are Family. Gerald bopped his head naturally to the beat.

Beep Beep

"We got signal!" Karma squealed. Then, for reasons known only to her, she dialed Detective Manuel's number.

"This is Manny," he answered.

"Hi. Uh, Detective? Uh, this is um, Carol." Karma, all of a sudden, was reduced to a nervous schoolgirl.

"I knew you'd call eventually," he said confidently.

Patricia grabbed the phone from her friend, irritated that she was acting so foolish over a boy.

"Hey! We have something for you. Steve Vickson. Remember him? Ball player, dog fighter? We found him. You got a pen?"

"I do. Go ahead."

Patricia gave him the coordinates, then explained what him and his guys would be walking into. She told him about the child and that they were taking him to the hospital. She never mentioned Robin. When he asked to speak to Carol again, she hung up, instead, telling Karma that he's an asshole and she shouldn't have called him.

Peppermint Patty turned and smacked Robin angrily across the unswollen side of her face, taking out her frustration on the innocent woman.

"Watch your fucking mouth around the child!" she said sharply, before returning to her seated position and staring out the window, still annoyed at her friend.

BZZZZ

Karma's phone vibrated. 'Patricia must've turned off the ringtone without her noticing,' she thought to herself. It was a text from Detective Manuel, 'call me when your momma ain't home.'

Karma smiled. Patty Brown was not her mom; Keisha Lucas was. *'IS!'* she thought to herself.

Karma still thought about her mother every single day. She still felt her love, her passion, her drive...

She still felt her strength as she fought right up until the very end, when her life was cut short by that evil man. Karma still heard the **POP!** from the pistol. The rancid odor of gunpowder still burned the inside of her nose as if it were yesterday. She still saw the horror in her dad's eyes as her mother ceased to exist in a flash. There one second, gone the next. It was a snuff film that played in her mind over and over on a loop.

Karma was on the couch watching Chopped when the doorbell rang. Her mom didn't answer because they were just about to crown the Chopped champion for that episode. Karma knew who'd won already, she'd seen the episode with her dad, Detective DeWayne Lucas, but didn't let her mom know. This was girl time. This was mommy and me time, and with Keisha's busy schedule, the only time they had together, uninterrupted. Except tonight, they were being interrupted.

"GODDAMNIT!" her mom yelled as the ringing continued, more urgently than before.

Karma heard her open the door, say, "What the hell... ?" Then the sound of glass breaking. Then, "KARMA, RUN!"

She didn't run, though, she was frozen with confusion. She sat still, as a man dragged her mom violently into the living room, threw her to the floor, then aimed a pistol at her, demanding them both to *"SAY YOUR PRAYERS!"*

Her mom fought with everything she had, but was no match for the much bigger and stronger man. He forced them into the garage, then made Keisha drive, while he rode in the backseat with Karma.

With all that was happening, Karma was still more shocked than scared. Everything was moving so fast, it left her completely confused. She wasn't afraid of the man for some reason. Even at that young age, she somehow understood that he didn't want to hurt either one of them. With all the fighting and yelling that her mom did, he never once hit her back or did anything to harm Karma. It was more bark than bite.

She remembered that the man seemed so sad as he spoke in a remorseful tone. He kept saying that he didn't do anything wrong and that the detective was the reason all of this was happening.

He made Keisha drive to an area that Karma had never been to, and brought them to a cliff that sat high above a lake. They passed a sign that said Lakeside Tower.

He forced her and her mom to sit with their legs hanging over the edge while he called her dad. She remembered thinking that her father was going to come and save them, and everything was going to be okay. She was so sure about it that she wasn't even afraid sitting there so high up above the water and the jagged, rocky shoreline.

When her dad arrived, the man started to act differently, something in him had changed. Also, the quick resolution that she'd anticipated turned into more of a negotiation. She remembered the impatience she felt as to why it was taking so long. Fear crept in, and was quickly replaced by absolute horror when another man appeared, shot her kidnapper, and kicked him over the cliff.

He was obviously a friend of her dad's, and after a brief moment of relief, the new guy took her and her mom as his hostage.

This guy was different than the last guy. This guy was pure evil. This guy stank of anger and violence. Everything about him just felt bad to Karma, she hated him instantly. He spoke in such an arrogant, condescending tone. She would never forget his voice. It still gave her chills thinking about it. Oddly enough, even though she'd looked straight at him, locked eyes with him, she couldn't remember his face. Now and then, she'd have flashes of an image, but could never quite put it all together.

When he shot her mom in the head at point blank range, she remembered how his demeanor was one of superiority. And when he handcuffed her dad to a tree, then stood there and gloated in the man's face, he acted as if this was just a normal day for him.

As he dragged Karma by the hair down the hill to his truck, he told her to stay quiet and he'd let her go. Scream, and he would tear out her vocal cords with his bare hands.

As he got into his vehicle, he told her to count to 1000 by two, without any mistakes, then go save her dad. If she made a mistake, she was to start again. He said if she did it wrong, he'd come back and chop off her fingers. Her young mind did as she was told, not realizing that there was no way that the man could know whether she'd counted correctly or not.

Just as he put his truck in gear, he asked her, "Do you believe in God, little girl?" He didn't wait for an answer, he just sped off.

When she finally finished her count, she ran back up to save her dad but was stopped in her tracks at the sight of her mom's nearly headless body. This was the image that was permanently tattooed in her memory. It took her breath away. She was so utterly and completely distraught that her brain couldn't process a response. There were so many bits and pieces of jumbled thoughts and confusing information attacking her senses from so many different angles that her young body just shut down. She looked up at her dad, blinked, then woke up in a hospital two days later with no knowledge of how she got there.

"Mom?" she cried out, looking around at the unfamiliar surroundings, trying to get her bearings. "Mom!" she called out again.

"Mom!" Gerald looked confused as Patricia tried to wrestle him away from his mother.

Karma snapped out of her memory and looked around. They were sitting in a hospital parking lot, and her friend, Patty, was in the backseat, trying to tear the boy away from his mother.

"NO!" Karma yelled, "NO!" She got out and walked around to the other side of the car. "NO! PATTY, GODDAMNIT, NO! WE ARE NOT SEPARATING THEM, NO!"

"He needs to be checked out, look at him!" Patricia countered.

"Then she goes and gets checked out with him. We are not separating them. That is not our job. This is not what we do!" Karma insisted.

"She's gonna tell."

"Tell what? That we saved her from an abusive husband? Look at her face, she needs help, they both do!" Karma wasn't asking Patty, she was telling her.

Patricia stopped and let the boy go back into the safety of his mother's arms, crying. She stared at Karma remorsefully, knowing that her friend was right.

"Fine," she said, sitting in the passenger seat, angry. "You got lucky," She said to Robin without looking back.

Karma pulled her car closer to the front door of the ER, helped the two out of the backseat, then watched as they disappeared inside.

"Good job, baby," the voice in her head said.

"Thanks, Mom."

Chapter 9: Dirty Dishes

Patricia heard the insistent buzzing of Karma's phone on the ride back to the station, where she was getting dropped off to pick up her car.

Karma pulled into the space next to it.

"Why are you parking? We're done for the day, right? I thought you were just dropping me off," Patricia asked, as she unbuckled her seatbelt.

"Yeah. I uh, just have to pee real quick," Karma replied, avoiding eye contact. "I'll text you..." she said, jogging off, then turning back to run over and hug her friend. "I'll text you in a little while, ok?"

Patricia stood with Karma's hands in hers, and looked in her friend's eyes, searching for anything, reassuring herself that everything was alright.

"Ok?" Karma asked again, fidgeting back and forth, doing the 'I gotta pee' dance.

"Ok, love," Patty finally responded, playfully holding onto Karma's hands longer than necessary when she tried to pull away.

"I… gotta… pee…" Karma said, trying to tug her hands away from Patricia's much stronger grip.

Patty finally let go with a laugh, said goodbye, and watched her friend 'Karen walk,' into the front doors of the police station.

With a loud sigh, she started her car, ready for the long ride home. She backed out of her spot and was about to pull into traffic when she was nearly hit by an obnoxiously large Jeep pulling into the parking lot. She watched through her rear-view mirror as Detective Manuel parked in a handicap spot, then got out and walked into the police station.

"Whatever," she said to herself, then drove home.

The first thing she noticed when she turned down the street was her husband's truck not parked in the driveway of their three bedroom, rambler style home. She glanced at her car's clock, thinking he should've been there, but didn't wonder where he'd gone.

She pulled into the garage and went inside, stopping in the kitchen to look around, noticing how empty and barren it felt. This was where she lived, but it wasn't her home. It was just another temporary situation in a life full of temporary situations.

Her husband Charles moved them from place to place over the years, and she had begun to notice that she'd grown tired of it.

Maybe it was work, or her age. Maybe it was just her body going through the natural changes a woman goes through when they reach a certain stage in life.

Maybe it was her husband's habits that never seemed to change. There were a lot of unspoken things in their relationship that she just never felt comfortable saying.

It was becoming harder and harder to hide her unhappiness.

She saw an unwashed frying pan and a few other dishes sitting in the sink. Irritated, she rinsed them off and then set them in the dishwasher.

She exhaled heavily while looking around for other chores that her husband had left for her, then decided that she could use a bath and a glass of wine.

She opened the refrigerator to get the bottle she'd been looking forward to drinking since last week, only to find it ¾ of the way empty.

"Breathe, Patricia..." she said to herself, "count to ten..."

"Hey, babe!" Charles Brown appeared in the kitchen, walking in from the garage. He was in a good mood, as he usually was when he went off on one of his 'getaways,' as he liked to call them. He was doing it more and more often. Where it used to be once or twice a year, it was now becoming every couple of months. It happened before, and if this pattern continued, she knew it meant they would be packing up and moving again.

She glared at him from across the room, infuriated. Neither of them spoke, they didn't need to. This particular type of conversation was done in silence, like they'd done many times before.

Her: Is your brain ok?

Him: Yes.

Her: Is it satisfied? Can we go back to normal?

Him: Yes.

Her: (looking down at the blood stains on his shirt and bandaged hand)You need to clean up.

Him: (Following her gaze at his clothing, then back up to her, with tears filling the corners of his eyes) I'm sorry!

Patricia held her arms open as her husband crossed the room and buried himself in her embrace. She loved him with everything in her soul. He was a kind, thoughtful, and loving man who struggled with his demons. He'd always treated her with the utmost respect and adoration, assuring her at every stage of their lives that she was his one and only love. An excellent provider and protector, he was the perfect husband. As the father of their 3 grown kids, he continuously proved that all of the World's Greatest Dad mugs that filled their cabinets through the years were well deserved.

But, as he tried to explain to her so many years ago, there was something in his brain that turned him into a monster. Never towards her, or the kids, but to any and everyone else.

With him being as loving and happy as he was with them, he was just as hateful and angry at all others with whom he felt had threatened their peaceful existence.

He, Charles, was a normal man. It was his brain that made him a sociopath.

She remembered a particular experience with the depth of cruelty that his brain was capable of.

She'd been dealing with alcoholism as a result of her troubled childhood, and Charles, of course, wanted to help her through it, which he did, thankfully, but it was a lot of hard work. He would often go to her AA meetings just to show his support and love.

One day, after earning her 1-year chip, she was giving her testimonial to her group when a man yelled, "Yeah, right!" from the back of the room, interrupting and embarrassing her to tears. Charles, of course, ran to her, comforted her, and she finished her speech, ironically finding her voice and becoming a stronger person because of it.

On the way home, Charles was not his normal self. He was quiet as he drove erratically in seemingly random directions. He drove through a quiet suburban neighborhood she'd never been to and pulled up behind a vehicle that stopped in front of a modest single level home. The man in the vehicle got out, just as Charles ran up and knocked him down with one punch.

"Wait! Take it! Take what you want!" the confused man, who thought he was being robbed, tried to hand over his wallet and keys.

"Charles, stop!" Patricia ran over to try and control her husband, grabbing at his shirt, before noticing that it was the rude man from the meeting that Charles was assaulting. She stopped trying to help.

"You remember her?" Charles asked calmly. Left hand on the man's throat, right hand on a pistol pressed into the guy's nose.

The man was terrified. His tear filled eyes darted back and forth, confused, looking from him to her.

"Do you remember her?" Charles asked again, shoving the pistol into the man's mouth.

He nodded his head frantically, 'yes'.

Charles hit him in the head with the gun. "Wrong answer!"

That moment always stood out to Patricia. It gave her insight into the irrationality of Charles's brain. It was actually the right answer, her husband chose not to hear it.

"Let's go!" Charles made the man stand, then forced him into the back seat of his own car. He tossed Patricia the keys and told her to drive to Spec's liquor store.

"What's your name? How long you been sober?" Charles asked.

"Mike," the frightened man answered, "Mike McPhe..."

Charles hit him with his gun. "How long?"

"6..." he stuttered. "6 years, two months, 21 days."

"Wow, see babe? It can be done. That's a long time, Mike. Good job. That's a lot of hard work. What did you drink? What was your poison?" Charles asked as they pulled into the parking lot.

"Um... uh..." The man looked around nervously.

Charles hit him again. "What's that? I never heard of Um uh. You babe? You ever heard of Um uh?"

Patricia shook her head, no. He was trying to include her in a conversation she wanted no part of.

"Jack!" Mike blurted out when Charles reached back to hit him again. "JACK DANIELS!"

"Hey, go get two bottles of Jack, please, love," Charles told his wife. She did, then returned and drove them around to the side of the building.

Charles opened the bottle and held it under Mike's nose.

"Remember this?" he mocked.

"Please... no. Please," the crying man begged. Patricia couldn't watch.

Charles poured some of it on his fingers and then spread it across the man's trembling lips. "Go ahead, you know you want some. Take a sip," he said quietly.

"No, please, don't make me. Please. I'm sorry. I'm so sorry, ma'am. I shouldn't have... I was trying to be the funny guy. I'm so sorry."

"You made my wife cry, Justin. Now DRINK!" Charles shoved the bottle in the man's mouth and tipped it over, causing him to cough and choke and spit it up.

"Please. Stop. I can't. If I drink, I die. Please!"

Charles put the gun to the man's head and pulled back the hammer. It was ready to fire.

Patricia put her hands over her ears, she couldn't bear to listen. She knew how hard it was to stop drinking, it was a daily struggle. This wasn't fair, the man had fought his demons and was winning. She could only hope to make it that long.

"Drink," Charles demanded.

Seconds of silence passed before Mike finally reached for the bottle, took a deep breath, then tipped it over and drank.

"Ahh." He let out a satisfying breath as he hung his head. It was the sound of familiarity. He looked up at Charles, a defeated man.

"More!" Charles demanded, pressing the gun harder into his temple.

Mike downed more than half of the bottle, burped, then finished the rest remorsefully.

"Satisfied?" he slurred.

"Babe, let's take him back," Charles said, "He's learned his lesson. Take the expressway."

Mike sat back. He shed the tears of a broken man. They were the tears of a man who had scratched and crawled to fight his addiction. He'd rebuilt his life, only to have it all taken away from him. His face begged the question, 'What's the point?'

Charles opened the second bottle and passed it to him, "More!"

The man took another humiliating swig and then began mumbling incoherently. He was drunk.

"Pull over," Charles told Patricia, as she navigated traffic.

"What? I can't just... We're on a bridge, I can't..." She started to say.

"Pull over, now! Just pull over," Charles demanded..

Patricia turned on her hazard lights, slowed, then pulled the car as close to the median as possible.

Charles looked at the drunk man and said, "Get out!"

"What? I can't get out here... I'll get hit..." Mike tried to say, looking panicked at the traffic whizzing by in both directions around them.

"GET OUT! NOW! GET OUT OF THE CAR!" Charles pulled the door handle, then started kicking and punching the man, "GET OUT!" forcing him out of the vehicle.

"Wait a minute... Wait, please!"

Cars honked angrily and tires squealed as drivers tried to avoid an accident.

"Good luck!" Charles said as he pushed a bottle into Mike's hand and pulled the door closed. "Babe, let's go!"

"WAIT!" he begged, horrified, as Patty pulled into traffic and drove away.

"I thought you'd be gone longer," Charles finally said, showing her the plastic bag he was holding.

"I drank your wine and was planning to replace it before you noticed. I made some of those fried egg cups you like, too. I was going to have the dishes done, so everything was perfect when you came home. I'm so sorry," he said as he embraced her and kissed her head and neck. "You stink," he laughed.

She was back where she needed to be emotionally.

"What happened to your hand?" she asked, noticing a bloody and poorly wrapped bandage across his palm.

"Oh, I cut it, it's nothing," he replied.

They showered together, and Charles made sure to get out first so he could greet her with a fresh towel when she was done.

They climbed into bed and laid peacefully, with her allowing him to watch ESPN, even though he would've been ok watching The Kitchen on Food Network. She stroked his head and thought about how she wished she could save him from himself. She knew he couldn't control his brain, no matter how hard he tried. Therapy was a waste of time, and the pills were a waste of money.

She was in love with a serial killer. She knew that his 'getaways' were just him out hurting somebody. Her perfect man had a flaw she couldn't fix, and it frustrated her as a woman not being able to help him.

Beep Beep Beep.

A text from Karma woke them up at 430 in the morning. 'CALL ME NOW!" all caps. Patricia's phone rang before she could reply.

"Hey... What's wrong?" she asked, concerned.

"She... she... she..." Karma was crying, unable to speak.

"What's wrong?" Patricia sat up. "Use your words!"

Karma cried frantically. "Celeste... she's dead. Celeste's been murdered!"

Chapter 10: She is not your babe

Patricia sat frozen on the end of her bed. She focused on her breathing, not wanting to let her mind wander. She didn't want the reality of what Karma said to affect her actions. She needed to be present for her friend, who sounded like she was in a bad place.

"Hey... where you going? You ok?" Charles woke up, genuinely concerned.

"It's Karma. Something happened." Patricia replied shortly.

Charles sat up and turned on the nightstand lamp. "Anything I can do?"

She didn't answer. After getting dressed, Patricia left and drove to meet Karma at the police station.

Karma was inconsolable. She was crying hysterically into Detective Manuel's shoulder when Patricia walked into the waiting room.

Patty reached for her friend and slid rudely in between the two, taking over as the woman's comforter with a dirty look for the detective.

"Shhhh I'm here, love, I'm here," the older woman stroked her friend's hair and rocked her gently, doing her best to be strong even as emotion dared to consume her as well.

"She... We just saw her yesterday," Karma cried. "She was just... We just talked, she was just..."

"Ok, love... let it out."

Karma went from crying to talking, back to crying. Detective Manuel left, then returned with a handful of tissues that Patricia angrily snatched from his hand. He attempted to reach out for Karma's arm, but was met with a death stare from Patty.

"Ok. You can go now," Patricia said harshly.

Detective Manuel looked at Patricia as innocently as he could, sensing the animosity.

Reaching out anyway to squeeze Karma's shoulder, he said, "I'm sorry for y'all's loss. I liked Celeste, she was my friend. I'm going to do everything I can to find the motherfucker who did this. I'm going upstairs now to start. I'll keep you posted." He looked at Patricia and touched her on the elbow. It was his olive branch. She relaxed her features and nodded a thank you.

"Babe, call me if you need anything," he said, walking away.

'Babe?' Patty thought. 'Who the fuck is babe? She is not your babe!'

"Ok, we get it..." Patricia said with all the attitude she needed to get her point across.

Karma picked up on her friend's energy and switched from sad to angry.

"Ok. Ok, alright," she said, backing away from her friend's grip and wiping her eyes. "We got work to do!"

She gathered herself, straightened her clothes, pulled her hair back into a ponytail, and took a breath. "Ready?" she asked. It was as much a statement as it was a question.

Patricia didn't have a chance to reply, Karma was already on her way through the glass door, headed towards the detective's area.

She slowed at an office that sat just past the elevators at the end of the hall, then paused and started crying again. Patricia caught up and saw what her friend was looking at. An organized desk with a neat stack of papers on its left, a neat stack of manila folders to the right, and a bunch of action figures in the middle as if a child had been playing there. Patricia didn't notice, but Karma saw Princess Leia, Captain Marvel, and Wonder Woman arranged in a way that had the three women standing victorious amongst the other random assortment of bad guy figurines.

"I didn't realize she had kids," Patricia said mournfully.

"She didn't," Karma replied before turning away, thinking, 'she did get the joke!' and walking purposefully into the office just beyond Celeste's.

"What do we got?" Karma said, interrupting Detective Manuel and another man as if she were one of the team.

"Hey, Hey! You can't be in here!" Both men instinctively reached for their guns before Detective Manuel let go of his and placed his hand on the other man's shoulder.

"Whoa, whoa... Hold on now, she's with me."

He shot Patricia a dirty look that Karma didn't notice, then said, "They're with me!"

"Hey, babe, this is my partner, Detective William. Detective, this is Carol Danvers and Diana Prince." He winked at Karma, who couldn't hide her smile.

"Oh. That's her, huh?" Detective William looked her up and down with an approving head nod, then reached his muscular arm across the table to greet them.

"Hello Carol, I've heard a lot about you. Nice to finally put a face to an... uh, name. Ha ha." Both men laughed. Peppermint Patty was not amused. The handsome face and the muscular physique might disarm some women, but it didn't impress her. She hated him immediately.

"And hello to you," he reached over to shake her hand. "I'm Detective William."

"I heard it when he said it!" she snapped. He wasn't going to get anywhere with that deep voice and fake charm.

He acted hurt.

"Look, cut the shit," Patricia said, "I'm sure that act works with all the girls, and if I was younger and desperate, I might've been lonely or drunk enough to teach you a thing or two, but you're a customer, etcetera.... A used car salesman at best. We didn't come here for you. My friends been murdered, so we can work together, or we can work without you, but cut the bullshit, ok? And use your regular voice, you're not fooling anybody!"

There was a moment of silence as they all mourned the loss of Detective William's ego. Detective Manuel did his best to hold in a laugh while Karma just stared in awe at her best friend. Detective William collected himself, then got down to business as if nothing had happened.

"So what we have here is the murder weapon, a large pocket knife with the handle broken off," he said. His voice was a few octaves higher than it was during his introduction. "Whoever did this will definitely have contusions on their hand. The M E on site could tell immediately that there were two different types of blood on that blade."

Patricia listened but could only focus on the man rubbing her friend's shoulder, consoling her.

Karma didn't mind. At all. She liked Detective Manuel, Manny, as she now finally called him. She never told Patricia all of the intimate details of their growing relationship, but then, Patricia had never said anything about hers either. She didn't have to explain that she actually did call him the night they met at the grocery store, and the conversation lasted all night. She didn't need to say that they continued it the next morning at IHOP over French toast and hash browns. She was probably moving too fast, but something just felt right to her. He was kind, thoughtful, and funny. He had a quick wit and came off as carefree until he spoke about something he was passionate about, then his voice changed, and his vocal cadence sped up so you could feel his energy. She never told Patricia that he only called her Karma in private. He called her Carol everywhere else... It was their little inside joke. She never had to say that the heart wants what the heart wants.

She hadn't felt this way in a long time. Not since Lee.

Karma knew she had messed up. She couldn't help being jealous. Lee was the perfect man. He was her soulmate... physically, emotionally, and mentally. He checked all the boxes, and she was with him at a time when she didn't believe that she was worthy of love.

But still, she couldn't help but look through his phone, or follow him to work to make sure that's where he was really going, or show up at the bars he was at when he was hanging out with his friends. She knew she was the problem, she just couldn't help herself. He was a man, men were not to be trusted... Everyone knew that.

On their last night together, they'd had drinks and played cards on her bed. They had a ridiculous movie playing on TV in the background, but neither paid any attention to it. He was tired from a long day at work, so she did everything to make him comfortable, including a sensual fingertip massage. He always loved the way she touched him, making him feel like it was her most important task at that time. She gave him her entire focus, pouring out every inch of love into her man. She knew he loved it when she would sit on his back and rub herself all over him. He told her that when she let her long hair fall down over him, it felt like a waterfall of love. Like he was being covered in a blanket of happiness. He'd said her massages woke up every single nerve ending in his body. The night was perfect, until it wasn't.

They kissed for a while, then he said he had to go home.

"Why?" she asked.

"I have a long day tomorrow, it would just be easier to leave from home instead of leaving from here. I didn't even bring my clothes," he said sleepily.

"No, you can just go from here," she said, feeling emotional.

"Not tonight, babe." He started to gather his things.

"NO! DON'T GO!" Karma started to cry.

"I'll be back tomorrow, Mama," Lee said, rubbing her leg.

"You're going to see someone else, ain't you? You're going to fuck some other bitch, huh?" she said, now angry. "Fuck you! GO THEN! GO, GET OUT! GET THE FUCK OUT!"

"What? No. Babe, don't," he said innocently.

"Ok… I'm sorry… It's just… You know I love you. I don't want you to go. I want you to hold me," she said, apologetically, her attitude changing once again.

"Tomorrow," he said, walking out the door.

She knew she was wrong, but she followed, in her nightgown, screaming at him the whole time, cussing, calling him names. When he got in his car, she got in hers, then chased after him, tailgating, swerving around him, cutting in front of him. When he parked, she pulled so close to his driver's side door that he had to get out on the passenger side. Karma ran over to him and spat in his face. Lee raised his hand to smack her, but didn't, he just turned and walked out of her life. Or as she knew to be true… He turned as she chased him out of her life.

"Hey, babe! Hellooo, Carol, you there?" Detective Manny asked, waving his hand in front of her face. "Hey, we have to go, can we talk later?"

"Huh?" she asked, snapping out of her memory.

"Don't go," she said before catching herself, "I mean... yeah, ok, we can talk later."

Chapter 11: Home Improvement

Patricia drove to the scene of the crime, and they were allowed to watch from outside the yellow tape. Karma was visibly rattled, but did her best to stay calm. Patricia cared about her friend, but her main concern was the crime scene. She was looking for clues or anything that might've tipped off the detectives as to who the killer was, but from the distance they were at, she couldn't see much. She suggested that they go get something to eat, then return later after everyone else had left.

Seven hours, four cups of coffee, and three bathroom trips later, the two women were finally able to walk around the scene where their friend took her last breath.

Karma stood at the edge of a blood stain, crying. Patricia walked around searching for anything that would solve a riddle she already knew the answer to, cursing herself quietly.

"AHHHHHH!" Karma let out a gut wrenching scream to the sky. "WHY!! ANSWER ME MUTHAFUCKA! WHY DO YOU KEEP TAKING PEOPLE FROM ME! WHY!" She fell to her knees, hysterical. "Why? Why does everybody leave me?"

Patricia ran over and embraced Karma, hugging her in a motherly way, doing her best to console her friend.

Karma buried her head in Patty's neck, then looked up and froze.

Patricia felt her go stiff and pulled away, "What? What's wrong?"

Karma's eyes were focused on something, and she moved quickly towards whatever it was.

"What, Karma? What?" Patricia asked.

"Look! There's something..." Karma let her words hang as she reached down to where the gravel met the dirt on the side of the road. "Look!"

Patricia stared in shock at the broken pocket knife handle that Karma was holding. It was engraved with the letters L E S. There was half of another letter before the L, that looked like it could be an R.

Two weeks later

Patricia looked over at Karma's phone as they rode down the street towards the post office. Both her screensaver and wallpaper were a picture of the 'Charles' knife. There were no other clues, this was all they had, and Karma was obsessed with it. Detective Manuel was, too.

"So he just left?" Patricia asked her friend.

"Yes, he just left," Karma said. "He said I was acting like a bitch and walked out!"

"He called you a b...?"

"Nooo, calm down. He said I was *acting* like one," Karma replied, sensing an explosion.

"I'm going to kill him," Peppermint Patty said under her breath.

Karma patted her hand, reassuring her friend that everything was ok. She explained how the detective had a lot going on. His ex-wife was harassing him, child support was killing him, and work was stressing him out. She made a point to say that he'd been going to his AA meetings and has been doing well since the incident where he broke every mirror in his apartment because she was taking too long to put on her makeup. She explained that what he really needed right now was her love and support.

"I was thinking about letting him move in, that way I can be there for him whenever he needs me... What do you think?" Karma asked cautiously.

Peppermint Patty had heard enough. She was seething with anger. She squeezed her mouth shut for fear that if she opened it, the words that flew out might do irreversible damage to their relationship. She decided right then that she was going to fix Karma's problem.

Karma parked, then ran inside to speak to one of her sources, who seemed to know everything about everyone in their little city. Patricia waited outside and did a Google search of Detective Manuel. She cursed herself for not doing it earlier, but she trusted her friend and felt that doing so was a violation of that trust.

It didn't take long to find his name and personal info, but before she could really dig in, Karma came skipping back to the car with a huge smile on her face. Patricia smiled back, happy that her friend was finally getting back to her old, silly, fun-loving self.

"Manny's coming to the party!" she squealed happily as she got in the driver's seat. "I'm so excited. Tonight's gonna be awesome, and I finally get to meet Charles! YYYYAAAAAYYY!. Her childish enthusiasm was addicting, and Patricia joined in Karma's little dance, as they both chanted, "Hey, Hey, Hey, Hey," in unison.

"Oh my God, I just realized... your husband's name is Charles. Like on the knife. You think they know each other? Ha ha. Like, all Charles are connected somehow? What if that really happened, where everyone who had the same name was connected in some way? What if you were connected to Patty Hurst? Or Patti LaBelle? Oh, what if you were connected to Patricia Heaton? Remember her from that one show? What was that show... Tim the Toolman Taylor was her husband! Remember? And there was a man that stood behind a fence. They never showed his face... There were kids on the show..."

"Karma! Stop," Patricia put her hand on the woman's arm. "Enough," she said, shaking her head with a smile.

"But, y'all could be..."

"No, we couldn't," Patricia interrupted.

"But..."

"Karma. No."

They both laughed as they drove off.

—-----------------------------------

Patricia was already at the very crowded, 80s-themed Halloween party when Karma and Detective Manuel arrived, dressed as Prince and Michael Jackson.

"HOME IMPROVEMENT!" Karma yelled, finishing her thought from their earlier conversation.

"Hey y'all," Patricia said, embracing her friend before shaking the detective's hand dismissively.

"Where's Charles?" Karma asked, looking around. "Oouu, girl, I love your costume, who did your dress?"

Patricia stepped back and posed, showing off her Wonder Woman outfit. "Donna, dahling," she said in a fake accent. "Mr. T went out to the car, he had a call from work. Those idiots can't do anything without him."

"I'm going to get a drink, do y'all want anything?" the detective said politely, excusing himself.

"We're already drunk," Karma said, then waited until he was out of earshot.

"Hey, listen," they both said at the same time.

"Jinx, buy me a Coke!" Karma laughed.

"No, for real, listen!" they spoke at the same time, again."

Karma talked over her friend. "There was a break in the case. He doesn't know I know, but I heard him say that they think they know who Charles is. Well, they at least have someone of interest that they're looking into. And get this, he's from Flowerton!" She paused for effect.

When Patricia didn't react, she continued, "THAT'S WHERE I'M FROM!"

Patricia felt hot as she tried her best to hide any emotion. She could feel her pores opening and beads of sweat beginning to form.

She looked around the room, hoping that Karma wouldn't notice her frantically searching for her husband.

"They think he's local." Karma continued, "I don't know how they figured that, but that's what I overheard him and Detective William saying earlier. We have to find his ass before they do! I'm going to remove that motherfucker from the planet!" Karma said excitedly.

"Ok," was all Patricia could manage. Her mind was in flight mode. She had to go. She had to find Charles, and they had to pack up and leave.

The front door opened, and she saw him. He was dressed as Mr. T, standing with a group of trick or treaters, laughing and smiling with other adults while the kids filled their bags with candy. Patty made a quick dash towards him before Karma could react, as she was facing the opposite direction.

"Hey, wait, where are…" was all she could get out before she lost sight of her friend. She found Patricia just as the woman grabbed Mr. T's arm and urgently pulled him away, leaving the party, but not before hearing the words that have haunted her existence since she was a child. Words that have lived rent free in her nightmares. Words that shook her to her soul. Her body went into shock. She stood frozen in absolute horror. Her best friend in the entire world just grabbed the man who was dressed like a 1980s sitcom character as he spoke to one of the trick or treaters, "Do you believe in God, little girl?"

Chapter 12: You knew!

Karma stood paralyzed, watching Patricia and Charles hurry to their vehicle, trying to get away. *'Get away...'* she thought, snapping out of her surprised state. "No! They're getting away!" Karma ran to her car, jumped in, and followed. She had so many emotions going through her head all at once. Justification being the strongest of all. She'd begun to think that maybe she did misremember the events of her mother's murder, as her dad said so many years ago.

'DAD!' she thought, picking up her phone and dialing his number. He needed to know that she did it;; she found the man who took her mom. Her. By herself. She finally did it. After all these years, she was finally worthy.

He didn't pick up.

Karma drove with laser-like focus. Her thoughts were on Charles and only Charles. Even as he seemed to be driving in a circle, it didn't matter. Even as she saw them pull over, still in the same neighborhood, then watched as Patricia got out and jogged away, her focus was still completely on Charles.

Ring Ring. It had to be her dad returning her call.

"Daddy!" she shrieked excitedly, before picking up her phone.

It was Patricia calling. Karma ignored it.

—----------------------

Peppermint Patty told her husband to let her out of the car after she explained that Detective Manuel was on to him. She told him that she would take care of everything while he,

Charles, went home to pack. She was angry. This is not what she wanted to happen. She liked her life here. She loved Karma and didn't want to leave her. Patty was sick of moving. It wasn't fair and she was pissed off, screaming at him as they drove!

"Let me help you," he tried to say, wanting to clean up his own mess.

She shot him a death look that said, 'you've done enough!' then got out and ran through backyards, back to the party.

As luck would have it, Detective Manuel stood outside alone, away from everyone else, smoking a cigarette. He had his back to her, and she snuck up silently from behind, knife in hand.

With the precision of a surgeon, she made a slice just above the back of his elbow, separating the tricep from the tendon, rendering his right arm useless, then with one hand around his mouth so he couldn't scream, she made 2 quick, non-fatal stabs into his abdomen.

"Stay quiet and fucking walk to your car!" she whispered as she felt his body slump, wanting to fall.

"What? Why?" The man was confused, but did as he was told.

Peppermint Patty reached into his pocket and grabbed his keys. Pushing him up against the car, she buried her knife into his thigh, then kicked it, driving the blade deeper into his leg, and let him fall as she dug around in his glovebox, finding a pair of handcuffs.

"You think you're so fucking smart don't you?" she growled at him. "You thought I wouldn't find out? I know who you really are, you lying piece of shit! WAKE UP!"

Detective Manuel had gone into shock, but a blow to the face from the butt of her gun, plus the taste of blood, brought him back to consciousness.

She got him into the car, then secured him to the handle of his rear passenger door.

"Where are we going?" He asked through broken teeth.

"You are going back to hell!"

Karma followed Charles to his and her best friend's house. It was a quiet, nondescript, middle class neighborhood. She pictured cookouts, where the men stood around talking about what type of lawn feed they used on their grass, while the women gossiped about who hadn't yet adopted a gluten-free diet for their families.

Karma wished she had a gun. She wished she had a plan. Hell, as long as she was making random wishes, she wished that she hadn't seen her best friend get in the same car as her mortal enemy!

"Only me…" she said to herself. "What are the fucking chances?"

Charles opened the garage but left his vehicle in the driveway, then hurriedly ran inside.

Patty would know what to do here. She always knew what to do.

'Wait a minute…' Karma thought to herself. 'Was Patty in on it the whole time? Did she know who I was and what he was this whole time? She was playing me! That fucking bitch!'

Karma's mind went in a thousand different directions, trying to remember situations that may have led her to this conclusion, but honestly couldn't find any. Either her friend really didn't know, or was an award-winning actress. Karma laughed at that thought. Patricia was no Angela Bassett… Peppermint Patty wore her heart on her sleeve, she couldn't hide her feelings. She *wouldn't* hide her feelings, she was much too…

Ring Ring! A call from her friend interrupted her thoughts.

"Hello?" Karma said distantly.

"Hey girl? Where you at? Did you leave the party? I'm with your boyfriend… We're wondering what happened to you." Patty asked.

"I'm at 2301 Hardies Ln," Karma replied.

Patricia was confused. "I have to tell you something about Manny... Wait, what? You're where? Why are you at my ...."

"I thought you were my friend," Karma said sadly, " you knew this whole time... You've been lying to me this whole time..."

"What? No! Wait, please, let me explain. Don't do anything, just wait! We're on our way!" Patricia said before the line went dead.

"Aaaaaaaahhhhh!" Peppermint Patty screamed, then turned and grabbed the knife that was still stuck in Detective Manny's leg, and re-stabbed him two more times. She stepped hard on the gas pedal towards her house, unsure of what she'd see when she got there.

If she knew her friend like she thought she did, Karma would've already called the authorities and would be happily showing everyone that she was a real detective, capturing a murderer, finally proving herself to her father. Patty suspected that her quiet little neighborhood would be flooded with the flashing lights of police cars, and news cameras would be interrupting her neighbor's sleep.

When she turned the corner onto her street, she realized that her thoughts were the exact opposite of what was actually happening. There were no lights, and no news team. Everything was quiet. She saw Karma's car, parked a few houses down from her own, but no Karma. She also saw that her garage door was open.

Patricia worried about her friend. She didn't want Karma to be subjected to the level of violence that Charles was capable of. Pulling into her driveway, she quietly got out and went into the garage for duct tape, which she used to secure Manny's mouth, as she pulled the bloodied man with her into the house.

The blood trail on the floor didn't surprise her. Nor did the broken, bloodstained 2 by 4 that lay near the door. What surprised her was seeing her unconscious husband seated at the kitchen table, duct taped, and beaten, with Karma sitting next to him, holding his pistol in one hand, while her other hand held a large kitchen knife.

Patricia approached carefully and sat Detective Manuel across from her husband.

"Karma...?" Patricia asked slowly, "What's going on, love? What are you doing?"

"Why is he here?" Karma returned, ignoring the question.

"Oh, he has something to tell you." Peppermint Patty slowly pulled the tape off his face, then smacked him hard. "Tell her!"

He spat blood, then in a broken voice said, "It wasn't a mistake. Our relationship... it was planned. I knew who you were. I worked for your dad when he was in Cleveland." He stopped, then restarted after another smack on the head. "OK, I was dirty. I was doing shit I wasn't supposed to be doing and your dad exposed me. He ruined my life... He ruined everything. I knew who you were when I saw you at the store. I recognized you, and I was planning to get your dad back by being with his daughter."

Karma stared at him, emotionless.

Patricia spoke. "I did some research. I saw him in an old photo. He was in one of the departments your dad consulted at."

Detective Manuel jumped in, "But I fell in love! I didn't plan to, but I did! Babe... help me... I love you."

"You don't get to feel love, you motherfucker!" Patricia growled.

POP!

She shot him in the face. His head exploded as he fell backwards in his chair.

Karma didn't flinch. "You knew..."

"Fuck, Karma, Celeste was my friend too!" Patricia pleaded. "I didn't know what to do. What was I supposed to do?"

"That's not what I'm talking about and you know it," Karma said plainly before exploding, "YOU FUCKING KNEW! YOU FUCKING KNEW! You lied to me for two years... I thought you were my friend." She began to sob loudly.

Patricia started to reach for her friend to comfort her, but Karma pulled back.

"What are you saying? I don't understand. Karma, what's going on?"

"HIM!" Karma pointed the gun she was holding at Charles, "HE'S THE ONE WHO KILLED MY MOM AND YOU KNEW THE WHOLE TIME!"

POP!

She accidentally pulled the trigger.

Chapter 13: Just let them pass

Time stood still. Neither woman moved. The only sound either of them heard was the ringing in their ears. Both stared wide-eyed at the hole in the wall. They held their shocked poses for what felt like minutes before they both yelled different things at the same time.

"WHAT THE FUCK!"

"OH MY GOD!"

The sound woke Charles up. He looked around confused, wondering why he was duct taped and bound, why his wife sat at the same table with a woman pointing a gun at him, and why the fuck, was there a headless man in his kitchen! He angrily yelled demands through the gag in his mouth, although neither woman paid any attention to him.

"I didn't mean to..." Karma explained innocently, "It just went off!"

"Put it down, Karma, before you actually hurt someone," Patricia said, holding out her hand.

"NO! I am going to hurt someone. I might hurt someones. Plural," Karma said matter of factly.

Patricia was stunned. She had a flash of anger, but calmed herself quickly. She felt bad for her friend. "Babe," she said, "I'm sooo sorry about your mom. I really am, but I had nothing to do with that, and I didn't know. I had no idea, I promise."

Karma searched her friend's eyes, wanting to believe her, desperate for the truth in what Patricia just said.

"But you knew about Celeste..." Karma asked.

"Not at first, but yes, I did," Patricia said remorsefully.

"AND YOU JUST..."

"Karma, listen, he's not perfect. He's done some bad things. Hell, we've done some bad things. He's got issues. I'm sorry about your mom, love, if I could change it, I would," Patty said, trying to keep her temperamental friend calm.

"Well, he's gonna die tonight, Mrs. Brown. And I'm going to be his killer," Karma countered, waving her gun around carelessly as she spoke.

"What good is that gonna do? Would your mom want you to kill..."

"Hell yes, she would!" Karma interrupted, "she would absolutely tell me to shoot this muthafucka! She would want me to avenge her..." Karma looked over at her friend, allowing the words to hang, waiting for the reaction they deserved.

Charles continued to furiously yell garbled demands to his wife as he fought to get free. The bulging veins in his forehead, an indicator of his efforts.

Karma wasn't worried though, there was no way he was getting out of his restraints. She'd learned how to tie someone down from the best, Mrs Patricia Brown, and her sociopathic alter ego, Peppermint Patty.

"SHUT UP! SHUT UP!" Karma yelled at Charles, jabbing him in the shoulder repeatedly with her knife.

"SHUT UP! SHUT THE FUCK UP! JUST SHUT THE FUCK UP!" She ended her last command with a pistol whip to the side of his head, and the gun pressed hard into the wound it had just opened.

"KARMA, ENOUGH! HE GETS IT! FUCK, YOU'RE GIVING ME A HEADACHE!" Patty stood, then seeing the hurt look on her friend's face, sat back down, rubbing her temples.

"Is his mom still alive?" Karma asked, calming down. "She raised a horrible fucking person. I think women like her should die. Is your mom still alive, Charles? Or did you kill her too? Huh? Mr. Charles Brown... Charlie Brown... Oh my God! CHARLIE BROWN! WHAT THE...? I JUST GOT IT!" Karma jumped out of her seat and started hopping up and down laughing, while singing, "Charlie Brown. He's a clown. Charlie Brown. He's a clown. Oh, and you're Peppermint Patty! I'm so dumb, I never put it together. Ha ha ha. That's so funny, I remember those stories! My mom used to read..."

POP!

The gun accidentally went off again. This time, shattering the glass of the microwave across the room.

Patricia took a deep breath before speaking. "Karma. Babe. Listen. You're my girl, you know that, but that's my husband. Right or wrong, I've accepted him for who he is, just as you've accepted me for who I am. We both know you're not a killer; you believe in justice. How bout instead of killing him, you just take him to jail, huh? How bout that? Imagine the headlines, 'Famous detective's daughter is a chip off the old block!' Think about how proud he'll be. You'll definitely make detective then!"

Karma paused, thinking about her dad and the fact that he never called her back. She scooted her chair closer to Charles and stuck the gun in his knife wounds, while laying her head on his other shoulder.

"Do you know how hard it was growing up? Do you know what you did to me? Do you actually know how fucking sad I was everyday? I was so lonely. Everyone I've ever loved has left me. Nobody loves me. Why doesn't anyone love me? Like, what the fuck?"

When Patricia reached out to touch her friend's hand, Karma pulled away, then stood. She wiped her eyes and said, "Fine, but he rides in the trunk!"

HONK! HONK! HONK!

"Karma, just let them pass!" A nervous Patricia said, holding onto the passenger side door in a death grip.

It was still dark on a rainy Monday morning, and early rush hour traffic, plus Karma's always erratic driving, had Patricia's anxiety at an all-time high. It didn't help that her husband was locked in the trunk on the way to be dropped off at jail.

It was a decision that weighed heavily on her heart, but after Celeste and now learning of Karma's mom, it was all just too much. Of course, she'd always known what he'd done, but she'd selfishly never personified any of the people they'd hurt. She intentionally chose to ignore the fact that all of them were someone's family member. They were all somebody's son or daughter. The hard truth was that Patricia is the narcissist she accused her husband of being. And this wasn't a revelation by any means. She was well aware of the things she was doing... She chose her path. But, as they say, karma was the universe's way of balancing things out.

Sending Charles to jail wasn't the ideal option, but to her friend, whose life was dedicated to bringing people to justice, it was the better choice. The only choice.

HONK! HONK! HONK!

The car behind them honked and flashed their high beams as if Karma had any control over the traffic in front of them. It reminded Patricia of a traffic incident she had with Charles years ago.

"I can't do anything! There's nowhere to pull over!" Karma insisted, holding her middle finger out the window. "Fuck you, asshole!"

Her car fought hard against the slick pavement. They could feel it hydroplane every time it hit a puddle.

"Karma! Just slow down! Goddamnit!" a terrified Patricia yelled.

The one lane roadway finally opened to two lanes each way, and the car behind them, an orange Mustang, pulled up alongside Karma's window. It slowed down long enough to hold out a middle finger at her, then pulled ahead, cutting them off, splashing water on the windshield, causing them to veer off the road.

"Bitch!" Karma stepped on the gas pedal.

"No! Please..." Patricia begged.

"I know that fucking car," Karma said, already full of the adrenaline from earlier. She raced to catch up. She drove recklessly, one-handed, sneering crazily as she gripped Charles's pistol in the other.

Patricia couldn't see her friend's intentions through her squeezed shut eyes, but she knew it wasn't good. "Karma... Please, love. Please slow down."

"I got you muthafucka," Karma said as she pulled up to the passenger side of the Mustang. With both hands already occupied, she made an awkward move to roll down her window, ready to shoot every bullet into the other vehicle.

POP!

Her third accidental shot went right through her left thigh.

POP!

The recoil from the gun caused her fourth to shatter the windshield. The car jerked right, hitting a guardrail, which sent them spinning, as the cars behind theirs slid on the wet pavement, smashing into them, flipping their vehicle over several times.

Karma's last memory was the taste of blood and an apology to her best friend in the entire world. "I'm so sorry, Peppermints. Can you forgive me?"

Chapter 13.5

"Oh. You're awake? Welcome back to the land of the living, my dear. I'm Nurse Becky. I've been taking care of you for the last 3 days. How are you feeling?"

A smiling nurse patted her hand gently.

"Thirsty," Karma said through a dry throat. Her entire body hurt. "What happened? I feel like I been hit by a truck."

"You were. Several, actually," Nurse Becky replied.

Karma's memory came back in a flash.

"Wait! My friend. Patricia. Is she ok? Where is she!" Karma tried to sit up but was held down by a back brace she couldn't see. Her body was heavily bandaged. Her right leg was in a cast. "There were other people in my car!" she said excitedly.

"As far as I know, you were the only one in that wreck. You're lucky to be alive," the nurse said, continuing to do her job, checking the monitors and filling out her charts. "Do you need anything? I'm going to have the doctor come in and check on you. Here's the TV remote and your phone. Press the red button if you need anything," the nurse said soothingly, before leaving.

Karma was confused. 'What happened to...?'

"Oh. I forgot. Someone left this for you." Nurse Becky came back in and handed her an overfilled, yellow shipping envelope.

Opening it immediately, Karma reached in and grabbed a Peppermint Pattie candy bar. Looking inside, she pulled out three figurines: a Wonder Woman, a Captain Marvel, and a Princess Leia, the same ones that they saw on Celeste's desk. There was a small tag on Wonder Woman's foot with the letters DC.

"You bitch," Karma whispered, smiling to herself.

The next item she pulled out was an Avenger's postcard that read, "Yes, I forgive you. Will you forgive me?"

"Of course," Karma cried, wiping her eyes. Finally, after taking a deep breath, she pulled out an old school iPod and its headphones. A sticky note attached said, Press play.

She was an emotional wreck by the time she put them over her ears, and there was no amount of tissues that would stop the flow of tears as Sister Sledge sang the chorus to their 1979 hit, "We are family. I got all my sisters and me."

THE END

Years later...

I used to think people were good. I remember how I used to think that even though people had different backgrounds, we were all the same. Sure, we've all made questionable decisions, but everyone was still generally good.

Maybe I was naïve, but I had always figured that all people wanted the same basic things, love, peace, and happiness. We all just wanted to raise our kids, be good neighbors, smile, laugh and have fun with our friends.

Remember that old story about the lady who steals bread to feed her starving kids? That woman wasn't a bad person; her choice wasn't the best, but that didn't make her 'bad'.

Like religion. At its core, all religions are basically the same. Be honest, be charitable, love thy neighbor, help when you can, do the right thing.

I used to believe that bad people were just misguided people, and if given the right tools, they would see the light and change.

Well, I was wrong.

Some people really are just bad. Some people just come out of the womb evil. It's crazy to think that there are actually human beings who feel good when they see others suffer. There are people who thrive on despair and sadness. Folks who are so selfish that they don't care how their actions affect anyone else. They torture helpless animals. They set fire to people's property. They inflict as much hurt and pain on innocent people as they can. They do bad just for the sake of doing bad.

And I know they know better. Everyone knows right from wrong, some people just choose wrong over right.

It took me a while to realize this, but once I did, it hit me like a ton of bricks. I remember feeling betrayed, like I'd been lied to. It was like learning that Santa Claus wasn't real, or that magicians weren't really magic, or that your dad wasn't your real dad...

But I digress.

As I sat on a bus headed upstate, every so often, I caught my reflection in the window. I saw the tired eyes of a man who's seen too much tragedy. I saw laugh lines etched in the skin of a man who's cried too many tears. I saw the look of determination on the face of a man who, through it all, has kept his promise to serve and protect those who can't protect themselves.

Hello, I'm Detective Dewayne Lucas. I'm the good guy.

-Excerpt from DETECTIVE LUCAS: END OF AN ERROR, Book 3 of the OVERKILLING THE PAST trilogy